All Books by Harper Lin

The Patisserie Mysteries
Macaron Murder: Book 1
Éclair Murder: Book 2
Baguette Murder: Book 3
Crêpe Murder: Book 4
Croissant Murder: Book 5
Crème Brûlée Murder: Book 6
Madeleine Murder: Book 7

The Emma Wild Mysteries
4-Book Holiday Series
Killer Christmas: Book 1
New Year's Slay: Book 2
Death of a Snowman: Book 3
Valentine's Victim: Book 4

The Wonder Cats Mysteries
A Hiss-tory of Magic: Book 1

www.HarperLin.com

Crème Brûlée Murder

A Patisserie Mystery

Book #6

by Harper Lin

This is a work of fiction. Names, characters, organizations, places, events, and incidents are either products of the author's imagination or are used fictitiously. Some street names and locations in Paris are real, and others are fictitious.

ISBN-13: 978-0992027988

ISBN-10: 0992027985

Contents

Recipes

Chapter 1

The cake made its grand entrance from the kitchen. Twenty-nine lit blue candles stuck out from all angles of the edible Eiffel Tower, giving off the effect that it was sparkling, like the real one did every hour on the hour after sundown. The cake added a bit of kitsch to the party, something lacking in typical Parisian social events, while the full-scale inspiration could be seen from the window of the Damour *salon de thé*, where the party was held.

Clémence beamed as two members of her staff pushed the big cake on a cart toward her. The guests began singing "Joyeux Anniversaire." Arthur, her boyfriend, squeezed her hand as she closed her eyes and made a wish before blowing the candles out. It was a challenge to do it in one breath, since the candles were all around the three-dimensional cake, and she laughed as she failed after multiple attempts. Arthur had to lift her up so she could blow out the candles at the top of the cake.

Her guests tittered in amusement, mock clapping, and Clémence never felt so connected to the close friends and family members who had shown up in response to her short-notice invitation. She hadn't wanted to celebrate her birthday, at first—her twenty-ninth year on earth wasn't a major milestone, and she was content to let it pass quietly as just another day—but she had finally been convinced by Arthur and her friends to do something. It made sense to throw something together at Damour, since the city's best desserts were already readily available.

Damour was a patisserie and *salon de thé* started by Clémence's parents, who were both bakers. Aside from the ones in Paris, they also had locations in Nice, Cannes, New York, London, Tokyo, and Hong Kong. Her parents were in Asia right now, working on the new store in Singapore. Their packaged chocolates, candies, tea, and drink mixes were also sold in gourmet supermarkets around the world. The name "Damour" was synonymous with gourmet desserts and treats.

The flagship location was at 4 Place du Trocadero, located in the 16th arrondissement, where Clémence worked most of the time inventing new dessert flavors and overseeing the store's operations. As the heiress of the family brand, she was technically in charge while her parents were away, although she relied on store managers, such as Caroline, to keep the three stores in Paris running smoothly.

Clémence's job came with plenty of perks, although the perks could be too much of a good thing sometimes. In the few months since she'd returned to Paris, after traveling around the world for two years, she'd gained seven pounds. Her metabolism wasn't what it used to be. But Clémence got to work with some of her favorite people everyday, her schedule was flexible, and she had privileges, such as closing the flagship store early on a Saturday night so that she could throw her private party.

All the chefs, bakers, apprentices, patisserie cashiers, and *salon de thé* servers from the Paris Damour locations were invited, but none were required to work, since Clémence had been considerate enough to hire a temp staff so they were free to enjoy the evening. It was as much of a celebration for the people in Clémence's life as it was for growing a year older.

Her aunt and uncle, who lived in Montmartre, came, but unfortunately Clémence's older brother, who lived in Deauville, had to go on a business trip to Scotland that weekend. Her sister, Marianne, who lived in the south of France, was on vacation in Italy with family but promised to visit or meet up somewhere with Clémence before summer was over.

After the guest had a nibble of the cake—which turned out to be white chocolate on the inside—Berenice Soulier, Clémence's friend and a fellow baker at Damour, took over the DJ table and put on her dance playlist.

All the tables in the *salon de thé* had been cleared off to the side just for this occasion. Some of the guests, already plied and loosened with champagne, began to dance. The others needed more alcohol before they could make fools of themselves.

"There's more champagne coming," Clémence told them.

Her friend Ben Mason began busting out cheesy dance moves such as the running man, the robot, and the electric slide, setting the silly tone for limb flailing-phobics to join in.

Sebastien Soulier and his girlfriend, Maya, joined in. Then Celine, a hostess at Damour, and some of the waiters followed.

As the evening went on, the guests got drunker and grooved harder. Toward the end, all shame was abandoned, and everyone really let loose. Dinner jackets were set aside, heels were taken off, and the impromptu dance floor had all their energy.

Clémence threw her hands up in the air, and she jumped around, heel-less. Her head buzzed from the champagne—she couldn't even recall how many glasses she'd drunk. She was stumbling into other guests—into Madeleine Seydoux and her boyfriend, Henri; Henri's brother Charles; and Cesar, Uncle Nicolas, and Aunt Juliette. Some of the waitstaff were doing the limbo, started by Jennifer, who was an American expat working as a patisserie cashier at the Damour St. Germain location.

Clémence stumbled into Arthur's arms. He was also buzzed by the high of the evening, and he actually danced even though he had two left feet, like most Frenchmen.

Arthur pulled her in for a slow dance, even though a manic electronic dance song was playing. She snuggled up to his shoulders, her nose touching his neck.

"This has been the best night," she murmured. "Thanks for talking me into this."

"It was worth it, seeing you do the moonwalk." He laughed.

They stayed that way for a moment, just the two of them, swaying drunkenly to the music. The dessert table at the side, which at the start of the evening was plentiful with Damour signature goodies such as macarons, tarts, éclairs, and crois-sants, looked as if it was hit by a hurricane. There were hardly anything left. They had a chocolate fountain, and all the fruits were nearly gone, as well.

Later on, Clémence was continuing to drink champagne. She felt so open and happy that she went around the room, hugging people and telling them all the gushy ways she liked them. When she was about to hug her aunt, she heard a woman's scream in the background.

Berenice cut the music.

The woman screamed again. All heads turned toward where it was coming from: *les toilettes*.

Maya came out of the door to the restrooms, her face as pale as meringue.

"What happened?" Sebastien rushed to her.

"D-dead," she croaked. "He's dead."

"Who's dead?" Clémence said.

"Cesar."

Clémence tried to snap out of her drunken stupor. Another dead body? She pulled Arthur's hand, and they both went into the restroom. They'd both seen enough dead bodies in the past few months to stomach this. Plus, since they were intoxicated, the event didn't feel quite real.

Clémence pulled on the door that opened to two more doors, one for the men's toilet and the other for the women's.

"He's in there." Maya pointed to the door, on which hung a line drawing of gentleman in a top hat. "I went into the men's room by accident."

Clémence took a deep breath and pulled the door open. There he was, slumped on the floor, hands grazing the toilet bowl. Cesar Laberg, Henri's brother and heir to the *Editions Laberg* publishing empire.

Chapter 2

*N*one of the guests were allowed to leave. Inspector Cyril St. Clair and his team started interrogating everyone.

Cyril headed straight for Clémence, who was in a corner next to the empty dessert table. She was staring off into space, contemplating what could've possibly happened tonight that caused Cesar to end up dead.

"For once," he said to her, "I would like to go a week without a Damour-related murder."

"You and me both," said Clémence.

Arthur came and wrapped his arm around Clémence's shoulders for moral support. "*Bonjour,*" he greeted the inspector stiffly.

"Dubois." Inspector nodded at him before turning back to Clémence. "So what is it, this time? Ransom? Blackmail? Why is that man dead?"

"I don't know," Clémence said sharply. "But I demand you keep your voice down. The victim is the brother of two of my guests. Please be sensitive."

"All right, fine." He lowered his voice. "But I still want to know, who is this guy, and what exactly happened here?"

It wasn't a total surprise that Cyril would question her first instead of the person who found the body, or the guests who knew Cesar better. Clémence had been inadvertently helping Cyril solve murder cases ever since she returned to Paris in the spring.

"His name is Cesar Laberg," she told him. "He's the heir of *Editions Laberg*. You heard of it?"

"The publishing company? Yes."

"Well, Cesar's the head of the magazine department now, and he was being primed to take over the whole empire."

"How do you know him?" Cyril asked.

"His youngest brother, Henri, is going out with a friend of mine, Madeleine Seydoux. You remember her?"

"Yes, of course." Cyril furrowed his brows in thought. "Hold on, I know these Laberg brothers. They're always on Paris Social's 'Most Eligible Bachelors' list."

Clémence gave him an odd but amused look. "You read that gossip site?"

"For work," Cyril quickly added. "For research purposes, of course. You socialites and rich people are always getting involved in scandals and murders. Of course it's something I *have* to keep up with."

Clémence snorted. "Sure. Well, I don't know much about the Labergs. I suppose you can question Henri or Charles Laberg."

They looked back at the brothers. Charles was on the phone, probably speaking with his parents, and Henri was being comforted by Madeleine in a tight embrace.

"Who found Cesar's body?" Cyril asked.

"Maya Diallo," she replied. "She's the date of one of my bakers."

Maya was on the opposite side of the room. Sebastien had his arms around her. She looked terrified. Clémence understood how shocking it could be to find a dead body. She'd stumbled across a few in the past few months.

"And what do you know about her?" Cyril asked. "This Maya Diallo?"

"Do you suspect her?" Clémence asked.

"I suspect everyone. Even you, too."

"We all know how well your suspicions have served you in the past," Clémence said sarcastically.

Arthur squeezed Clémence's shoulder. "Let's all calm down. We don't know what happened. We don't even know if Cesar was murdered."

Cyril waved him away. "How did Maya find the body?"

"She was going to the restroom," Clémence said, "and she had a little too much to drink, so she went into the men's room by mistake and found the body slumped around the toilet."

"Uh huh." Cyril scribbled this down in his little notepad. "How well do you know her?"

"This is the first time I've met her," Clémence said. "Like I said, she's Sebastien's girlfriend."

"So you don't know her well, then," Cyril said.

"No." Clémence was losing patience. "But I seriously doubt she had anything to do with this. She was screaming when she found him."

"Likely story," Cyril muttered. "Let's go see the body."

Clémence led him to *les toilettes.* The door was already opened, and Cesar's body was still in there, unmoved.

"*Excusez-moi, les gars,*" Cyril said to the members of his team. Some of them were collecting evidence, and a forensic photographer was snapping photos. He spoke to a member of his team, a man in his forties with round glasses that made him look like an owl. "What did you find out so far?"

"We don't know. No indication of foul play. We have to do an autopsy."

"Cause of death unknown," Cyril muttered. "What was he doing before he went into the restroom?" He turned to Clémence. "You have cameras here, right?"

"Yes," Clémence replied. "Hidden in the two chandeliers, if you recall."

"After I interrogate some of these witnesses, I want to see those tapes."

"I'll call my guy," said Clémence.

She had Ralph Lemoine on speed dial. Ralph worked at the surveillance company Damour used. Watching the store tapes had helped them with cases in the past. It was past midnight, but it was a Saturday, so there was a chance that Ralph was up.

On the third ring, Ralph picked up. "Clémence Damour?" he answered in a groggy but flirtatious voice.

"*Bonsoir*, Ralph. Sorry to wake you." Clémence explained that had been yet another murder. "Is it okay if we come look at the surveillance footage now?"

"Wait, you're saying somebody died at your birthday party?" He sounded more awake this time.

"Yes," she replied. "We don't know if he'd been murdered, but we'd like to see what happened to him leading up to his death, if possible, on surveillance."

"I'm up now, and I live close to work, so you can come by. I'll meet you there. What exactly happened?"

"I'll fill you in when we get there. Unfortunately, that annoying inspector is going to come. Hope you don't mind."

"I don't mind him."

"That makes one of us."

Ralph chuckled. "I'll start getting the footage ready for you, then."

"*Merci. À tout de suite.*"

Clémence hung up and saw Cyril St. Clair inter-rogating Henri Laberg.

"My brother doesn't have any health issues that I know of," Henri was saying. "He had seasonal allergies, but nothing that would kill him."

"Are you sure there's nothing else?" Cyril asked.

"Well, he was a little allergic to cats."

"Excuse me," Clémence cut in. "Sorry to interrupt, Henri. Cyril?" She pulled him aside. "I'm heading over to the surveillance place with Arthur first. Then you can join me once you've finished."

"Seriously, Damour? You get a head start on questioning the witnesses and now you get to go through the videos first?"

"It's not a competition," Clémence exclaimed. "Although, for the last case, I still haven't received my letter as part of my win."

Clémence and Cyril had made a deal that if Clémence solved the last murder case, Cyril would write her a letter of defeat for her to frame, expressing how she was superior to him in every way. So far, he'd yet to write it.

"It's lost in the mail," said Cyril.

"A deal's a deal." Clémence crossed her arms.

Cyril sighed. "Fine. Yes, okay. I haven't had the time. I've been busy. So busy that I can't even get any decent sleep on the weekends. Some Saturday this is turning out to be."

"Yes. It's not as if I want to be investigating another murder during my birthday celebration either, Cyril."

And yet, she was.

Chapter 3

Clémence thought it would be faster to take the Métro to the 15th arrondissement. Taxis were scarce on Saturday night. It was only a few stops away, and the Métro was open until around one thirty a.m. on weekends.

Even though it was August, it still got chilly at night, so Clémence and Arthur put on their jackets and left. Unfortunately, the guests had to stay until later, but Clémence couldn't worry about them now. Berenice and Sebastien, as well as the Damour store manager, Caroline, agreed to help keep things under control.

However, the Métro stalled near the Bir-Hakeim station. They were taking Line 6, which was above ground, and the train was sitting on a bridge over the Seine. On one side, they could see the Eiffel Tower, all lit up. Clémence could tell who the tourists were by whoever was impressed with the sight of the tower. Even though she saw *la Tour* practically every day, she was still taken with the view, but she couldn't enjoy it that night. She had too much on her mind, and she was too impatient to get moving.

"Why can't this Métro move already?" she muttered to Arthur.

"What a crazy night," Arthur said. "I can't believe Cesar is dead. I just talked to him ten minutes before he went to the restroom."

"*C'est très bizarre*," Clémence agreed. "And you know what? If it did turn out to be a murder, guess who's responsible? One of the guests at my party!"

Arthur frowned. "Not necessarily. How many guests were there? Forty? Forty-five?"

"Forty-four. Plus the catering crew."

"But you only know a quarter of the guests really well. The others are employees from other Damour locations that you barely interact with, and guests of guests."

"That's true, but it still doesn't make me feel any less responsible." Clémence sighed and tucked a strand of her dark bob from her face. "I wonder what happened? Who would want Cesar dead? A guy our age with no health problems to speak of doesn't just fall dead."

"Maybe he had a drug problem," Arthur said. "Didn't he look a little haggard to you?"

"I guess, but all the Laberg brothers have dark under-eye circles. It's probably genetic. Could it have been alcohol poisoning?"

"It's a possibility, I suppose," Arthur said. "But when I talked to him, he didn't seem that drunk, not more so than I was."

"What if it was suicide?" Clémence asked.

"Why would Cesar want to kill himself? He's young. He's successful. He's got everything."

"What makes a person happy is different for everyone. We don't know much about this guy. I have to find out more. The police have taken over, but I don't think tonight's the right time to investigate, since everyone's in shock and quite emotional at the moment."

"Here we go again," Arthur said.

The train jerked to life, and Clémence practically fell out of her chair. She was still a little drunk.

"I still can't believe there's another murder so soon after the last one," Clémence said. "And on my birthday? We were supposed to get completely wasted and spend all of our Sunday eating hangover food."

"We can still eat hangover food," Arthur said. "In fact, I'm craving a hamburger right now."

"I wish there was more street food in Paris like there is in the States. Where's a hot dog cart when you need it?"

They got off at Métro La Motte-Picquet to change to Line 10 to Métro Avenue Emile Zola.

When they got to the surveillance place, Ralph was already there, and he opened the door as soon as Clémence rang.

Ralph was in a clean white dress shirt and dark denim. In his early thirties, he usually had scruffy facial hair, but he was clean shaven that night, making his dimples more prominent when he smiled.

"*Bonsoir*, Ralph," Clémence said. "This is my boyfriend, Arthur. I don't think you've met."

"Hi." Arthur stuck out his hand.

"No." Ralph's smile dropped as they shook hands. "I don't believe we've met."

The two men took a moment to size each other up. They were dressed alike. With his jacket off, Arthur was also in a white shirt, with black dress pants. His sleeves were rolled up, and his chestnut-colored hair was nicely gelled.

"Come on in," Ralph said. "Oh, and happy birthday, Clémence. Why didn't you invite me?"

"Oh, I'm sorry." Clémence smiled apologetically. "I didn't think you'd want to come. Next time."

"Of course I'd want to come. I'd go to any party at Damour. It looked like a fun night." Ralph sat down in front of one of the many screens. "Feel free to pull up some chairs next to me. I've already rewound to the start of the evening. What is it that you're looking for?"

Clémence and Arthur sat on either side of Ralph. "I'll point out the victim. His name is Cesar Laberg."

"Laberg," Ralph said. "I know that name. Why does it sound familiar?"

"He's a publishing heir."

"Oh." It struck Ralph. "Of *Editions Laberg*?"

"Yes," Arthur said dully.

"I know them," Ralph exclaimed. "They've published some of my favorite books by Agnes Belrose."

"Oh, you're a fan of Agnes Belrose, too?" Clémence exclaimed.

"Yes, *Le Port* is still my favorite book of all time. What about you?"

"*Le Port* is great, but *Les Belles Filles* is the best, in my opinion. I don't know how she does it. The characters are so sad, but I laugh on every page."

Arthur cleared his throat. "Maybe we could save the book club discussions for later. There might be a potential murderer on the loose."

"Oh, you're right," Clémence said.

Ralph rolled the video. The two cameras in the chandeliers showed everything from an aerial point of view. Clémence watched as the guests came in at the start of the evening. The hired waitstaff from a catering company had already set everything up. Two of them took the guests' jackets, and three of them circulated the room holding trays of champagne flutes for the guests to take to get the evening started.

Clémence watched for Cesar, but he must've arrived fashionably late. She did recall that Henri and Madeleine had been among the first to arrive, and Cesar and Charles among the last. Clémence didn't know Henri's older brothers that well, but Madeleine had told her they wanted to come because they were huge fans of Damour macarons. Plus, they wanted to meet beautiful women.

There were certainly beautiful women there. Celine, who was close with Clémence, was a cute blonde with a rotating door of boyfriends. Adi and Melanie were Clémence's friends from lycée, and the other Damour staff were all adorable in Clémence's eyes.

Cesar certainly knew how to charm the ladies. He had a crowd of them around him a few times throughout the evening. Charles Laberg was chatting up a storm with Celine by the end of the night. Clémence knew Celine well, and she guessed Celine was probably smitten, even though Celine's intense infatuations never lasted longer than a few weeks.

Clémence remembered being introduced to Cesar, as she scrutinized the video footage of them chatting after they greeted each other with *bisous* on the cheeks. He had dark, almost black hair, with hazel eyes that were almost golden. He was the tallest and the most well built of the Laberg brothers. Dressed in a fitted grey Armani suit, he exuded confidence and charm. Not only that, he was apparently a brilliant businessman. Cesar was managing the magazine department for now, but he had a lot of intelligent things to say about the French literary scene. He told Clémence that he intended to follow his father's legacy in discovering and publishing many of France's bright literary talents. Clémence remembered being impressed by Cesar.

Clémence had already known Henri through Madeleine. He was a nice guy, if a bit lazy. Charles was more carefree and outgoing, and he mingled with everyone just as well as Cesar throughout the evening. He was less serious than his older brother, was less shy than his younger brother, and was one of the first to join in with Ben on the dance floor.

When she'd questioned Henri and Charles after they discovered Cesar's body, they were both in shock. Neither knew what had happened. She couldn't broach the subject of mental illness at the time, especially with the ambulance sirens sounding in the distance.

The only thing she could do now was to see what Cesar had been up to the hour before his death. Clémence noted all the people he talked to. At one point, he looked to be in an intense discussion with Maya, before walking away. She walked back to Sebastien.

Did they know each other? Maya had only started dating Sebastien recently. They had been introduced by a mutual friend. Paris was a small town in many ways. It was possible that she'd known Cesar before the party.

Cesar had drunk four glasses of champagne. He had eaten one caramel éclair, a piece of opéra cake, six macarons, and a crème brûlée. Madeleine wasn't kidding when she said Cesar was a fan of Damour desserts.

Cesar had just finished the crème brûlée before going to the restroom.

The doorbell rang. Ralph paused and went to the door. Inspector Cyril St. Clair entered. He looked pale, with dark under-eye circles. It was probably way past his bedtime.

"You're done questioning all the witnesses?" Clémence asked.

"Mademoiselle, I have people for that," he said pompously. "I have a whole team at my disposal."

"Right. Then how come I'm the one doing all the real work?" Clémence muttered.

Cyril ignored her. "What have you found out so far?"

"We were just watching what Cesar was doing before he went to the restroom."

Ralph rewound the video, and Cyril watched as Cesar leaned against one of the walls, scraping the ramekin with a spoon. When he finished his crème brûlée, he gave the empty ramekin to a server and walked to the restroom. Naturally, there were no cameras in there, so they couldn't see what happened.

"So," Cyril said. "The man ate one of your crème brûlées and he dropped dead."

Clémence sighed. "That's what it looks like."

Chapter 4

"There's nothing wrong with my crème brûlées," Clémence insisted. "If the ones at the party were harmful, most of my guests would have dropped dead by now. My head baker made them himself, just hours before the party."

"Sebastien made them?" Arthur asked.

"Yes. We don't usually sell crème brûlées in the patisseries, but once in a while, we make them in special flavors for the *salon de thé*, so they're a special treat."

"What kind of crème brûlée was the victim eating then?" the inspector asked.

"I don't know," Clémence said. "I believe Sebastien made them in lavender, orange, and classic vanilla."

"And Sebastien is Maya's boyfriend?" Cyril asked. "The woman who discovered Cesar's body?"

"Yes," Clémence replied. "They've been dating for a few weeks. Don't tell me you suspect Sebastien now. I've known him for years."

"Besides, one of the servers was walking around with a desert tray, and Cesar picked the crème brûlée himself," Ralph added. "It's not like anyone gave it to him specifically."

"Let's watch that footage," Cyril said.

Ralph rewound until he found the moment where a tall, wiry, nondescript waiter with short dark hair passed by with the tray, and Cesar didn't look as if he needed much thinking before taking the ramekin and a spoon. Cesar dug into it almost immediately.

"We don't know if there's even anything wrong with the crème brûlée," Clémence said. "Sure, Cesar goes to the restroom right after and dies, but say the crème brûlée *was* poisoned or something, would the effect be this immediate?"

"We don't know how long it took for Cesar to die," Arthur said. "Maya discovered him, what, ten minutes later?"

"It's possible he was poisoned," Cyril said. "We'll find out after the autopsy. *On verra.* We'll see." He stood up and buttoned his Burberry jacket and turned to leave.

"Wait, that's it?" Clémence asked.

"There's nothing else we can do in the meantime while we wait for the results," Cyril said. "I suggest you go home."

The front door closed with a clang.

Clémence turned to Ralph. "Can I get a copy of the tapes from this evening?"

"Sure." Ralph gave her a flirtatious smile. "I can make a DVD and drop it off at Damour tomorrow, if you're open."

"We probably will be," Clémence. "I talked to my parents earlier, and they want the store open. *Merci.* I really appreciate it."

Arthur scowled at him, as he stood up and followed Clémence out the door.

Out on the street, they had to call a taxi company for a pickup because the Métros had stopped running.

As they waited, Arthur turned to her. "I don't like the way that Ralph was flirting with you tonight."

Clémence played dumb. "Was he?"

"The way he was looking at you, even when I was there."

"Oh. You weren't jealous, were you?"

"Jealous?" Arthur huffed. "I'm talking about respect."

"So you've never flirted with a girl while her boyfriend was there in your playboy days?"

Arthur thought about it. "Only when I thought the girl deserved better."

"Ha! I knew it. All men are slime."

"So this surveillance guy thinks he's better than me? Please."

"You're blowing things out of proportion," Clémence tried to say gently. "Some guys just like to flirt."

"So you knew he was flirting. And you flirted back."

She rolled her eyes. "Come on. Don't be that way. All you need to know is that I don't have an interest in Ralph romantically. I don't even know him that well."

Arthur took a deep breath as the taxi came. "All right. You're right. Forget it."

"We have way bigger things to worry about than whether some guy was flirting with me or not." Clémence leaned on his shoulder in the backseat to show that she wasn't mad. "And it's not to our disadvantage. He's helping us."

"Your company's paying him to work for you. He has to help you either way."

Clémence shot him a look.

He kissed her forehead. "Yeah, I know. I'm sorry you didn't have a better birthday."

Clémence laughed. "Don't worry. I'm used to this type of thing by now."

"Geez, maybe it's a bad idea to be open this morning," Clémence muttered to herself. Her bright blue eyes were fixed on the door of *les toilettes*. It was almost opening hour. The hired catering crew had helped clean up the night before, and her staff had done the rest.

Since there was no evidence of foul play, the police didn't think Damour was a crime scene. Clémence's parents, who were still in Singapore, had agreed with Caroline, the head manager, that the store should stay open. Clémence didn't think so, but she understood their reasoning. If Damour closed, it would've meant something was wrong. They were lucky enough as it was that no paparazzi had been around in the middle of the night. At one a.m., the tourists had also gone, and there were few witnesses to the police cars except the neighboring staff of other cafés and restaurants.

News might break sooner or later that Cesar Laberg had died in Damour's men's room, but business was business. It wasn't as if anybody at Damour was responsible for Cesar's death...wasn't it?

However, Clémence did feel guilty about the whole thing. A murder wasn't a fun way to end a party. And it didn't feel right to let customers use the men's room when it had recently hosted a fresh corpse. She made the executive decision to put an "out of order" sign, and she made the women's toilet unisex.

Clémence told Caroline what she'd done before heading back to the kitchen, where Sebastien and Berenice were working at one table. The brother and sister were both making éclairs, piping the cream filling into the choux pastry.

"How's Maya?" Clémence asked Sebastien. "She seemed a bit traumatized last night."

Sebastien shook his head. "She's probably sleeping in right now, because she couldn't really fall asleep after all the madness yesterday evening."

"Poor girl," Berenice said. "She comes out to meet your friends for the first time and finds a stranger's dead body near a toilet bowl."

"Maya knew Cesar, actually," Sebastien said.

Clémence's ears perked up. "How?"

"They used to work together. He was her boss."

"At *Editions Laberg*?"

"Yes. She was working at a magazine there," Sebastien said. "She was the editor of a new cooking magazine, and it folded."

"Oh. Where's she working now?"

"She's a book publicist now," Berenice said.

"Berenice would know," Sebastien said. "She spoke to Maya every chance she got—interrogating her throughout the evening, practically."

"I wasn't interrogating." Berenice pointed a wooden spoon at him. "I'm just trying to get to know my future sister-in-law."

"Oh, come on," Sebastien said. "Sometimes you act more like my grandmother than my sister. Why would you assume that we're getting married?"

"You're in your thirties," Berenice said. "Despite your youthful appearance."

"Hey, I just turned thirty."

"Please. You're about to turn thirty-one in September."

"That's not old," Sebastien said. "People aren't marrying until much later now."

"Except I think you're the kind of guy who needs to get married," Berenice insisted. "You live alone, and God knows what you do puttering around on your days off. Maya seems really grounded. She'll help you get out of your shell. We worry about you, you know. I'm glad you finally found someone."

"I was doing well on my own," Sebastien said defensively. "I'm head baker at the top patisserie in Paris, aren't I?" He must've thought about Maya again, because a small smile broke out on his face. "Maya is pretty great, isn't she?"

"Look at you." Berenice laughed. "You're so in love. I've never seen you this way, this...euphoric."

"It's a disease, isn't it?" he said. "I can't believe I'm acting like one of those saps."

"I can't believe you made me think you were gay all this time," Berenice exclaimed.

"You just came to that assumption yourself." Sebastien grinned mischievously. "But thanks for the support. It means a lot."

"I didn't know your girlfriend worked in publishing," Clémence said, who wanted to steer the conversation back to the subject.

"Yeah." He smiled dreamily. "She has a passion for anything to do with the written word. She's quite driven."

Clémence's head was already turning. She planned on meeting Madeleine Seydoux later that day, because she figured Madeleine would probably know more about Cesar's background. It wasn't an opportune time to talk to the grieving family members, so she had to go to the next best thing; she wanted to wait a day to speak to the Labergs out of respect.

Now that Clémence knew Maya used to work for Cesar, Maya would be a good person to interrogate.

"How well did Maya know Cesar?" she asked Sebastien. "How close were they?"

"I don't think they were friends or anything. They had a professional relationship. They hadn't been working together all that long. He was only her boss for a few months, I think. Maya said it was fortunate the magazine folded, because she wanted to be a publicist anyway."

"I wonder if she'd be interested in being Ben's publicist one day," Berenice said. "You know, after he finishes his novel. Is she good?"

"Her clientele is building every day," Sebastien said.

"Did she change jobs recently?" Clémence asked.

"In February," he replied.

"You think I can meet up with her?" Clémence asked. "I don't know what happened to Cesar, but if it was murder, maybe she'd know something."

"Clémence, you think everything's a murder these days," Berenice said. "I don't blame you. But what if it wasn't?"

"I hope that's the case. But past experiences have taught me to hope for the best and prepare for the worst. I want to gather information in case it is a murder. I mean, there's a pretty good chance it is, as much as I hate to admit it. A young man like him, rich, powerful, good-looking—he was probably the envy of many people. It wouldn't hurt to gather information. I feel responsible, since it happened at my party. Maybe Maya could tell me if he had any enemies."

"Maya can certainly help," Sebastien said.

What if the killer *was* Maya?

Clémence berated herself for turning into Inspector Cyril St. Clair, but she couldn't help it.

Chapter 5

As much as Clémence hated to admit it, the inspector was right to have his suspicions. Maya did find Cesar's body.

Although there hadn't been a scratch on him. No wounds, no blood, just a limp body. A clever murderer wouldn't put herself at the scene of the crime like that. Or had Maya just been pretending to be distraught?

Clémence sighed. She was thinking the way Cyril did when he accused Clémence of killing her building's caretaker when Clémence discovered the old woman's body. Just because Maya found Cesar didn't mean she did it. But why had she been in the men's room? Could it be explained by simple intoxication? Or did something else happen in there?

Sebastien had given Maya a call, but it went to voicemail, so he left a message saying that Clémence was interested in coming by and asking her some questions.

Clémence took down her information from Sebastien, and after wolfing down a tuna baguette sandwich for lunch, she left for her new mission.

The paparazzi had been scarce lately, and she hardly encountered them anymore. In August, many Parisians were on vacation. It left the city quieter, and it was also a month when films were made here. A big blockbuster sequel was currently being shot in central Paris. She knew Hollywood A-listers were in town to make the action film, and no doubt the paparazzi were much more interested in them than her, a dessert heiress who already had her fifteen minutes of fame in a kidnapping attempt.

Thank goodness her time in the limelight, or whatever it was, was over. She could go back to her daily routine, running errands—or solving murders—around the city without worrying about the tabloids and blogs scrutinizing whether she looked good without makeup or where she got her shoes. Clémence wasn't cut out to be a celebrity, however minor.

She took the Métro to the 10th arrondissement. Maya's office was north of Gare du Nord.

Sebastien guessed that Maya was out for a business lunch, probably with an author, which was what she did often. After Sebastien gave her the contacts for Maya's company, she'd tried calling the office, but she got the voicemail, probably because it was lunchtime. Clémence didn't mind going to Maya's office to wait for her. If Maya turned out to be out for the entire day, Clémence would just hop over to Madeleine's workplace to speak to her instead.

She followed the map on her phone to a run-down Haussmanian building. The office was on the fourth floor, and Clémence walked up the creaky old stairs. There were two doors, and she pushed open the one on the right to see a receptionist.

The young woman had fire engine red hair that came from a bottle and wore vintage cat-eye glasses. "Can I help you?" she asked.

"Yes, I'm here to see Maya."

"She's actually lunching with a client right now." She typed into her computer. "Do you have an appointment?"

"No, but we're friends. It's a personal meeting about something important. Do you know when Maya will be back?"

The young woman regarded her with interest. She had a wide mouth, with coral lipstick that clashed with her hair applied to her thin lips. "You can wait for her. Maya should be back soon. She doesn't have a meeting until three p.m., so she should be free when she comes back."

"Great. *Merci.*" Clémence sat down on one of the chairs.

"I'm Daphne, by the way."

"Clémence. *Enchantée.*"

The office was decorated in a modern barnyard chic style, with its glass tables with tree trunk legs, fluffy white carpeting, and pale blue wooden chairs with purposely chipped paint. A nature motif ran throughout the décor and wall art.

Daphne tilted her head and examined her. "You look familiar."

Clémence tried to brush it off. "People are always saying I look like somebody. I must have one of those faces."

Daphne seemed like the type to read gossip blogs and tabloids. Clémence hoped she didn't recognize her. Luckily, she didn't seem to.

"How long have you been friends with Maya?" Daphne asked.

Clémence surmised that she was probably bored stiff at her office job most of the time, and wanted to chat—gossip. She figured she could use this to her advantage. "I met her only recently," Clémence replied. "She's dating a friend of mine."

"Ah, the guy who comes around, who's always smiling?" she asked.

Sebastien now had a reputation for constantly smiling? Clémence chuckled at the thought of the new Seb and how much he'd changed recently. How love could transform a person.

"Yes," Clémence said. "He's a good friend of mine. I don't know Maya too well, but she seems really nice. It's impressive what she's accomplished. Do you know she used to work at a culinary magazine?"

"Right, before she came to work here." Daphne nodded, pity blatant in her expression. "Poor thing, getting fired before she could really make a name for herself."

"Fired?" Clémence frowned. "I didn't know that."

"Oh yeah. She'd worked her way up at this magazine, ever since she interned while she was still in university. Last year she finally got a shot at her dream job of being the editor. Can you imagine? Being an editor of a nationwide magazine at thirty? Anyway, the magazine folds as soon as the boss's son takes over. She wanted to work at another magazine, but that Laberg guy just wouldn't give her a break."

"Why not?"

"I don't know. But he sounds pretty awful. She says he's an arrogant asshole, so I guess they didn't get along. Then she started working here. She seems pretty content at this job."

"Wow. That sucks." Clémence took it all in. Sebastien had said that Maya changed careers because she wanted to, not because she was fired. Maya must've lied. What else did she lie about?

If Maya hated Cesar, she didn't act like it at the party. She was smiling the entire time, even when she was talking to him.

Just then Clémence's phone rang. It was Inspector Cyril St. Clair.

"Excuse me," she said to Daphne, and she went outside to take the call. "Cyril?"

"Damour," he replied. "I've got news."

"What is it?" Clémence asked breathily.

"Your friend, Cesar Laberg? Well, he committed suicide."

"*What?*"

"Yes. We got the blood test back, and he'd taken antidepressant. His psychiatrist confirmed that he'd prescribed them. Cesar had overdosed, taking the toxic dose."

"So he was depressed? Really?"

"Yes. Not only that, this morning, his mother found a suicide letter in his study."

"Did Cesar live alone?"

"His family owns a mansion in Neuilly-sur-Seine. Cesar still lived at the family home, and he had half a floor to himself."

"What did the suicide letter say?" Clémence asked.

"It's quite a logical letter. Not very emotional at all, but practical. It was more of a will, listing what he wanted to give away to people."

"Can I see the letter?"

Inspector Cyril St. Clair sputtered. "Do you think I'm working for you? No, you can't see this letter. The only reason I'm even calling you is to tell you that it was a suicide so you could stop whatever snooping you're doing at the moment."

"Do you even know if the letter's real?" Clémence said.

"His family recognized his writing," he shot back defensively.

"Yes, but handwriting can be faked. Have you taken it in for a graphology test?"

"It's real," he protested. Clémence heard him take a deep breath. "But yes, I did plan on submitting it for a test."

"Sure you did," Clémence muttered under her breath.

"*Pardon?*"

"Where did you find the letter?"

"Enough, Damour. This case is closed. Caesar Laberg had a case of depression nobody knew about. He was prescribed pills, and he took one too many at your birthday party. Maybe because he was drunk. Who knows what this guy was thinking? The rich are always messed up. I really suspected he had a coke problem at first. But we figured it out, and that's that. He committed suicide, and that's the bottom line."

He hung up. Clémence walked around the hallway, thinking. Cesar Laberg committed suicide? It was plausible. She hadn't known him too well, and she would have no idea what kind of demons he had. *Maybe I should just forget about meeting Maya and go home.* At least she didn't have to mull over which one of her guests was a murderer.

As she turned to go back inside to tell Daphne that she was going to go, she heard footsteps coming from the bottom of the staircase. Clémence looked down and saw Maya's curly dark hair. For the party, Maya had a bold Afro, but today she had it styled into a poufy bun on top of her head.

Maya was originally from Guinea. She had coffee-colored skin, full lips, and dark, almond-shaped eyes. As Maya neared the fourth floor, Clémence saw that she was wearing bold hot pink blazer and electric blue glasses. At her party, Maya had looked more like Diana Ross, in a classy silver dress, but today, she looked every bit of the hip young professional working in the publishing industry.

She looked up and noticed Clémence. "Hey, Clémence?"

"Maya, *salut*." Clémence greeted her with *bisous* on the cheeks. "I'm here to see you."

"I just got Sebastien's message when I was walking back to the office. Come on in to my office."

Before Clémence could protest, Maya ushered her in. Clémence figured it wouldn't hurt to talk to Maya and possibly get more information about Cesar in case she ever needed it.

Maya's office kept in line with the barnyard chic decor. The light green walls gave the room an air of serenity. On the wall above her desk was photography triptych of tree bark, branches, and leaves. Her desk was a huge slab of wood with metal legs. Only a silver MacBook and a minimalist silver lamp were on her desk.

"I love the decor," Clémence said. "My mom would approve. She's very into interior design."

"Thank you! I'm liking it too." Maya closed the door. "My coworkers are total minimalists, and I guess I've adapted to their tastes. Please sit down. What did you want to talk to me about?"

"It's about Cesar Laberg."

Maya nodded. She took off her glasses. It left ridges on the sides of her nose. "I kind of figured."

"I hope you've recovered from that evening. I know it wasn't exactly a conventional party."

"It was definitely a shock." Maya sighed. "The police grilled me for hours. Then I had a total breakdown and cried because I was so tired. I asked for a lawyer because they seemed to find it more suspect that I was crying. Sunday, I kind of just spent the day inside, trying to pull myself together for the workweek."

"Well, the—"

"Clémence, I heard from Sebastien that you're good at solving crimes. I figure you're probably trying to gather information about Cesar and his death."

"Yes, but—"

"Do you suspect me? Because I don't blame you if you do. The police does. I haven't heard from them yet, although they're supposed to go through my lawyer at this point. But I had nothing to do with Cesar's death, despite what it seems. What do you want to know about us? That Cesar and I worked together, and that he fired me? Yes, we didn't get along, but I would never kill him! Never."

Maya's expression contorted into one of pain. Clémence thought she was on the verge of crying.

Before she could reassure her and tell her what the inspector had found out, Maya spoke up again.

"It's true that I hated him. I'll lay it all on the table now. I'd been working at Laberg since I was in university. I'd always wanted to be the editor of a magazine. I was lucky enough to get an internship at *Bon Goût*. Who doesn't love food?"

"I remember that magazine," Clémence said, nodding. "It was great. I think they even did a feature on my parents years ago."

"Right. I think it was when I first started interning. That's when I learned to write about articles about food, chefs, and restaurants, and it turned out that I was good at it. When I graduated, I got hired as an editorial assistant. I did the usual assistant tasks, and they gave me small writing jobs, like short restaurant reviews or chef profiles. Then I managed the blog portion of the website. Three years ago, I got promoted to a features writer. It was fantastic, and I was over the moon. Fast forward two years, and I'm promoted to editor. Editor at twenty-nine. Not bad, right? Well. Then Cesar Laberg took over the magazine department." Maya rubbed her eyes underneath her glasses.

"Did you have to work with Cesar all the time?"

"I'd known him for a while, since we all work in the same building. He'd been working in another department while I was moving up the ranks through the years. Our paths did cross sometimes, like at company parties, events. Sometimes at restaurants for lunch. I never liked him. He was arrogant, kind of obnoxious, and he only got his position through nepotism, which I couldn't stand."

Clémence inwardly cringed. She had often been accused of nepotism, herself. Her parents were successful bakers and business owners. Damour was a huge success in France and in major cities around the world. She was an heiress who would inherit all this someday with her older brother and sister. In the meanwhile, she had one of the best jobs in the industry. She made creative decisions all day, inventing dessert flavors and helping her bakers make macarons and pastries when they needed extra help.

"He would hit on me, too," Maya continued. "At first, he'd just flirt, but after a while, he started asking me out all the time. I just wasn't interested. He had a reputation. He dated quite a lot of girls at the company and left them heartbroken. I didn't want to go through that. Besides. I didn't find him attractive. He was too self-righteous and self-entitled. I even told him that when he kept persisting on taking me out for drinks. I prefer someone more quiet and sweet, like Sebastien. Anyway, Cesar took over the magazine department and said he was shutting down *Bon Goût*. Many of us got laid off. To say that I was disappointed would be an understatement. I tried to apply for other jobs at the magazine, even lower positions, but I found that I was kind of blacklisted. Or at least that's how it felt like."

"You think Cesar blacklisted you at the company?" Clémence asked.

"Maybe. Maybe it was revenge for rejecting him all these years and bruising his ego. He could get any girl he wanted and probably wasn't used to rejection. I tried applying for editorial jobs at other magazines, but the only good offer I got was at a tabloid. I turned them down, and luckily, I found a good job here. I still miss writing for a magazine, but I love helping authors, and nurturing their careers. Sometimes I do freelance on the side at magazines, so I'm getting the best of both worlds, really." Maya took off her glasses and looked Clémence in the eyes. "I'm telling you all this because I want to lay it all on the table. Yes, my relations with Cesar hasn't been all that great, but I certainly didn't have anything to do with his death."

Clémence nodded, taking it all in. "How did he react to seeing you at the party?"

Maya shook her head at the memory. "At first, he was pleasant. He shook Sebastien's hand and made chitchat with us. Then he got drunker throughout the evening and a bit nastier. He made a snide remark about Sebastien when we were alone. Then he launched into this whole tirade of how I had bad taste in men, and that I was probably just a lesbian using Sebastien for social leverage because I was a nobody. I was so angry. I was fuming. I tried to calm down. Sebastien was engaged in another conversation, and I just downed a glass of champagne and tried to let the anger go. But I couldn't. I needed to give that Cesar a piece of my mind, especially after the fiasco with the job. I wanted to tell him that he was a vengeful, talentless jerk. I looked around and tried to find him, but he wasn't around, so I figured he was in the men's room, and I went to look for him. The men's room was, curiously, not locked. The door was slightly ajar. That's what I told the police, and it's the truth."

"Well, you did tell me that you were going in there to use the restroom," Clémence said.

"It's true. I did lie about the fact that I went into the men's room by accident. I didn't want to get in trouble with the police, and I panicked. So I made up that lie. Because I *really* didn't have anything to do with Cesar's death. All I wanted to do was confront him. I never imagined he'd be dead. I checked his pulse, so my fingerprints would probably be found on him, and I told the police that. Otherwise, I didn't lay a finger on him. All I wanted was to give him a piece of my mind, but someone beat me to that and more." Maya began to get teary and she buried her face in her hands.

Clémence had heard enough. "The inspector said Cesar might've killed himself. He said they found a suicide note, but he didn't exactly tell me what it said. He mentioned it was more like a will."

Maya looked up at her through her parted, tear-stained fingers. "Suicide?"

"Yeah. He overdosed on antidepressants, and it turns out that he had depression."

"Wow." Maya sat back.

"Did Cesar seem like the kind of person who was depressed?"

Maya slowly shook her head. "No. I don't know. He was always doing things for attention. Partying like crazy and coming in on Mondays hung over. He had girls coming and going through a rotating door. It could explain some things. Depressed people sometimes do look for instant gratification to fill a void, right?"

"Right," Clémence said. "He sounds like a rock star."

"I guess I never thought he had anything to be depressed about," Maya said. "He could do anything he wanted. He could buy anything he wanted and have anybody he wanted, almost."

"I'm not sure if I completely buy the fact that he committed suicide," Clémence said. "I mean, it sounds like there are people out there who might hate him and resent him. But what if it wasn't a suicide? What if someone made it look like one? And what if the letter wasn't a suicide letter, but just a will? I'm just trying to look at this from all angles here."

"Yes. I don't know. It doesn't look good, either way."

"What would make more sense to you though, Maya?" Clémence asked. "Cesar killing himself because of depression, or somebody murdering him?"

Maya looked down at her desk, at the paper-weight in the shape of a golden egg. When she looked up at Clémence, there seemed to be a glimmer of certainty in her eyes.

"Somebody murdering him," she replied.

Chapter 6

*A*rthur worked near Métro Miromesnil, and since his consulting company was on the way back to the patisserie, she made plans to meet with him for lunch. She waited for him in the lobby of the building.

Arthur came out of the elevator and smiled. His chestnut hair was growing out, and it was parted and neatly gelled with an adorable wave at the front. After they kissed and stepped out onto the street, his brown eyes shone with a golden tinge under the sunlight. They went to a nearby *crêperie*, where Clémence ordered a spinach and goat cheese galette and Arthur a seafood bisque galette.

"How's it going at your new job?" Clémence asked. "Are you feeling withdrawal from university life?"

Arthur shook his head and laughed. "Not at all. Aside from seeing my prof, it could get pretty solitary working at the library. Hey, why didn't you ever visit me there?"

Clémence reached across the table to pinch his cheeks. "You're such a whiner. I would've if your snotty school would let me in without a student ID."

"I was so lonely," Arthur joked.

"Didn't you have any friends at school?" Clémence teased.

"Sort of. But I was an older student, and the other PhD students were kind of aloof and not interested in making friends. Not that I was, either. I am glad I'm working now, since it can more be more of a social environment."

"I feel the same about working at the patisserie. I don't think I can be a painter full time. I need to interact with people."

"Which is why I'm liking the job," Arthur said. "I look up to my boss. He's not as pompous as other successful men, and he's quite flexible, letting us take breaks and extended lunches when we want as long as we get the work done. Right now, we're working on rebranding the XY clothing store."

XY was a clothing chain, a French version of The Gap. It had been popular when Clémence was a teen, but in the last decade they had trouble staying relevant.

"You're involved in fashion?" Clémence was amused.

"I'll have you know I'm quite fashionable."

She had to admit, he did know how to dress reasonably well, although it was in the most classical, preppy sense. All the bourgeois men dressed more or less the same; style was like a uniform with men and women alike in Paris. "But this is a women's store."

"I think you forget that I have two sisters, and one of them is in fashion school in Italy to become a designer."

"Right," Clémence said. "That's true. We'll see how it goes. Make me proud."

"I'll be sure to consult you on the latest trends."

"I'll try," Clémence said. "I'll wear what I have to look good, and I am known to shop on occasion, but I don't really keep up with the latest collections."

"Not even now that you're back on the socialite scene and you have friends in fashion?"

"I'm not back on the socialite scene," Clémence protested. "I'm just happy the gossip blogs are leaving me alone. Now I can wear the same pair of pants three days in a row without feeling like a criminal."

Their food came. Clémence dug right in; she was starved. All she had for breakfast was a *pain au chocolat* from Damour, and while it was full of butter, chocolate, and greasy goodness, it was low on nutrients.

Arthur chuckled at the thought of something. "You know, there's one thing I really don't miss about school—the unisex restrooms. I had to listen to the girls talk about the most inane things. Hair and boys and lip gloss. Ugh."

Clémence chuckled. "You should hang out in the back kitchen at Damour. It's pretty much what Berenice, Celine, and I talk about."

"Do you talk about me?"

"Always. You and murder cases."

"Right, the murders. So what exactly is going on with the Cesar Laberg case? Have you heard anything from the police?"

She sighed and explained what the inspector had said, and her visit with Maya. Arthur took it in as he finished his galette.

"What do you think?" Clémence asked. "Murder or suicide?"

"I'm not surprised by anything these days," Arthur said. "But I don't know. I had maybe a half-hour conversation with Cesar about the World Cup. He seemed like a pretty fun guy. Why would he kill himself?"

"Was he drunk when you guys talked? I only chatted with him a bit when we were introduced. I didn't pay much attention to him throughout the evening."

"Not *drunk* drunk. He seemed really easygoing, the kind who enjoyed life. I don't know if it makes sense he'd commit suicide."

Clémence shrugged. "I knew a girl who committed suicide when I was studying in America. She lived on my floor in the dorms. I didn't know her well, but I think she was bipolar. Sometimes, I'd see her at parties, extremely happy and dancing like everyone else, always either high or drunk. Other times I'd see her looking glum and bored, listening to music with headphones on at the library. Once I even caught her crying to herself at a table where she was studying. I'd thought it was the pressure of winter exams. Then during the spring semester, she slashed her wrists, and her roommate found her."

"Maybe you should talk to the people who did know Caesar well."

"One step ahead of you," she said. "I've left a message on Madeleine's phone. I want to see if she can get me invited over to her boyfriend's house. That way, I can talk to everyone in the family at once—the parents, both brothers, and maybe even the servants. I'll be able to find out what this letter said. I think if I just keep asking questions, even about things that seem insignificant, I might get something out of it."

"It doesn't hurt," Arthur said. "But what about leaving the case to the police this time? Did that ever occur to you?"

"Is that a joke?"

He smiled and shrugged. "Sort of."

"I wish I could trust them enough to, but I feel responsible, since Cesar did die at my party. I need to get to the bottom of this."

"And you will. But once you do, let's take that vacation we were talking about. Most of the Parisians have abandoned the city, and I want to join them."

"Maybe if I take a break from Paris, I could take a break from all these murders."

Arthur chuckled and held her hand on the table. "Let's hope."

Chapter 7

"*L*ift those legs!"

Clémence and Berenice reluctantly obeyed their boot camp instructor. This was Clémence's first outdoor workout class, and it felt like death.

"Higher! Higher!"

If I go any higher, I'm going to pull a groin muscle, Clémence thought.

They were working out on a patch of grass outside the Louvre. Berenice had been faithful to these workout sessions, coming twice a week. At first Clémence had been concerned about working out in public in case the paparazzi got wind of her, but she figured now that her fifteen minutes of fame was up, she could go back to doing whatever embarrassing things she wanted to in public. A part of her really enjoyed being bullied by a sadist into getting into better shape.

The pounds she'd gained since she started working at the patisseries again all went straight to her hips. She was now restricting how many sweets she was putting in her body, but it wasn't easy, considering she was surrounded by them every day. Her mother used to have the same problem, but she developed a habit of eating rabbit food and exercising six days a week, early in the morning. Clémence wasn't ready to make that level of commitment yet, but the masochism of boot camp workouts was a good start.

"Push-ups! Come on. I need fifteen push-ups, now!"

Clémence didn't know how to do one push-up, never mind fifteen. Their instructor was a short but bulky Spanish man in his early thirties with square sideburns and amazing hair that was slick and styled into a pompadour.

She resigned herself to doing girly push-ups, with her knees on the grass. She had to build up her upper body strength.

"Come on, Clémence, you can do better than that! Faster. Stop scowling. Smile. Smile through the pain!"

Smile through the pain? Clémence found the suggestion ridiculous, but she did it anyway. Soon she was laughing. Berenice couldn't help but laugh, too. There were only three other girls in the class, two of whom were super fit and ran rings around them twice while Clémence and Berenice lagged behind, panting and complaining.

There were fifteen minutes left in the class, as Clémence could see from her sports watch that also measured her heartbeat. She did lunges and sit-ups, jumping jacks and butt squats. When they were done, Clémence and Berenice fell on the grass in exhaustion. It was a particularly hot afternoon. Clémence squirted water all over her face and neck.

The instructor smiled, dropping his drill sergeant act as he packed up. "Good job, girls."

"I can't feel my legs," Clémence moaned.

"Sorry about that, girls," he said brightly. "Take a bath. That helps the muscles. À *la prochaine fois!*"

"Yeah, see you next time." Berenice sat up and looked around. "Man, it's so nice to be working out outside, at least. Gyms are so depressing."

Clémence sat up, too. A girl in a straw fedora snapped her camera phone in their direction. Clémence wondered if she was going to appear sweaty and makeup-less on some gossip site again, but the girl could've been a tourist. They were surrounded by beauty. Everybody was taking photos.

Before it became one of the biggest museums in the world, the Louvre used to be the royal palace. Clémence admired the sculptural details of the Louvre palace's façade, contrasted against the modern glass pyramid, which was designed by I.M. Pei in the eighties.

Clémence used to visit the Louvre to draw all the time when she was younger. She'd take a stool, her sketchpad, and pencils, and find a different wing every time to work in. She drew everything from sculptures to windows to people looking at paintings. It was a quiet, reflexive experience, almost meditative, as she would be so absorbed in the act of drawing that no thought entered her head except for those related to observing and transferring what she saw onto paper.

She loved those days at the Louvre by herself. It was a shame she hadn't been back inside the museum since she returned to Paris from traveling the world for two years, but she'd like to. She could buy an annual membership again. Of course, there were too many tourists in August to go during the day, but perhaps Wednesday evenings were a possibility, since the museum was open until nine forty-five p.m., and the crowd was different. She didn't know why they were different, but they were. There were fewer tourists who only wanted to document the experience with their high-tech cameras, and more who were introspective about art, looking at each piece slowly and prudently, as if everything was an experience to savor.

"I wish I had to time to go to the Louvre this week to start drawing again," she said with a sigh as she slowly sat up, too.

"Why don't you?" Berenice turned to her. "You used to go all the time, didn't you?"

"Yeah. It was nice to do something for myself. Especially now that Arthur's living with me, and I'm constantly busy with the patisserie, and all this murder stuff, it would be great to start it up again."

"I thought you said there's a good chance that Cesar committed suicide." Berenice shook her head. "I can't imagine someone wanting to do that. Especially in a dramatic way. He must've wanted attention, even for his death, as though being one of the most eligible bachelors in France wasn't enough."

"That's what I want to confirm tonight. I'm going to the Laberg family house in Neuilly to talk to everyone. Madeleine got me an invite to dinner."

"Dinner? Oh, fancy. I heard they have an amazing mansion. I saw it once in *Elle Decor*. If I were you, I'd be ecstatic."

Clémence stretched, trying to reach her toes with her fingers. "I'm not sure if 'fun' would be the word I'd use to describe how I think this evening will go. After all, I'm going to be broaching some serious subjects. I'm going to have to find some palatable ways to ask, 'What kind of depression did your son have?' and 'What did he write in his suicide letter?'"

"Hmm, yeah, true. Good luck."

"Thanks."

The girls carefully stood up. Clémence felt her sore muscles pulsating and she couldn't wait to go home and take that bath already. They took a walk through the Tuileries first, where people were eating lunch, chatting, or napping in the green chairs. Little kids poked wooden boats with sticks in the fountains.

There were all kinds of flowers and lush trees on either side of them as they walked toward the Luxor Obelisk. Clémence appreciated the simple beauty and joy of the garden, knowing that as soon as she exited, there would be cars and traffic and people to face again.

Chapter 8

*S*ince Arthur hadn't been invited to dinner at the Labergs' with her, Clémence got ready alone. She wore an emerald green wrap dress, courtesy of her designer friend Marcus Savin. It was simply the most comfortable dress she'd ever worn, with the silk-and-cotton blend soft to the touch. With a black Chanel clutch and basic black Louboutin heels, she was ready to mingle with the bourgeois.

"Don't burn the place down," Clémence told Arthur.

"I won't." He kissed her good-bye. "*Bonne chance.*"

She playfully ruffled his hair and then left. Whenever she went to somebody's home, she made sure to bring something from Damour. But since Cesar died after eating crème brûlée from her *salon de thé*, she wasn't sure it would be sensitive to bring one of their desserts.

At a flower shop, she bought a lovely bouquet of pink roses. She checked her watch. She had plenty of time. It wouldn't be difficult to find a taxi as she walked closer to Place du Trocadéro.

"Where to, mademoiselle?" the cab driver asked.

"Neuilly-sur-Seine, *s'il vous plait*." She gave him the exact address after retrieving it from her smartphone.

Neuilly was just on the outskirts of Paris, an area composed of rich residential neighborhoods. It was above the Bois de Boulogne, and was close to the 16th, so Clémence arrived in no time at all.

"*Merci, monsieur.*" Clémence slammed the door shut after paying him. The taxi drove away, leaving her alone before a three-story mansion with a vast garden. It was gated, and Clémence had to buzz for them to let her in.

The mansion was estimated to be sixty million euros, according to Berenice. It had twenty rooms, and the floors were served by two lifts. The ground floor had high, modern windows that probably gave a great view of the gardens, which was supposed to have been inspired by the work of André Le Nôtre, the landscape architect behind the gardens of Palais Versailles and the Tuileries.

Clémence heard there was a pool, too, which was probably in the back. No wonder the Laberg brothers still lived at home, even though they each had their own apartments in central Paris. The family mansion had live-in help, and the boys must've been waited on hand and foot. The

Labergs made Arthur's family seem middle class in comparison.

The front door opened, and the head of an older gentleman poked out first, followed by his lanky, uniformed body.

"*Bonsoir*," Clémence greeted him with a polite smile.

"Mademoiselle Damour?" he asked in a grave tone.

"*Oui.*"

"Come in."

He made no introductions, but Clémence could tell that he was one of the many help in the house.

"May I take your purse?" He gestured to her quilted leather clutch.

"Um, sure." She took out her smartphone and slipped it into one of the pockets of her dress. It bulged from her upper thigh beneath the fabric, but she liked to have her phone close to her in case she needed to take photos of anything.

The interior of the house, as expected, was grand in every sense of the word. High ceilings, Louis IX furniture, chandeliers, gilded mirrors. It was like a modernized version of a small palace.

Clémence was shown into the salon, where Madeleine, Henri, and Charles were already sitting with drinks in hand.

They all rose to greet her with *bisous*.

"I just heard that you were joining us," Charles said.

"Yes," Clémence said. "I hope it's all right. After what happened at my own birthday party, I wanted to pay you a visit."

"Of course it's all right. Glad to have you." A drink table with crystal decanters and countless bottles of expensive alcohol was by Charles's side. "Would you like a drink?"

"Sure," Clémence said. "Maybe a scotch on the rocks."

"Is that your drink of choice?" Henri smiled at her.

"Whenever I'm with boys, I drink like the boys," Clémence said.

"And here I am with my girly rosé," Madeleine said.

Henri and Charles had the same nose as Cesar, strong and slightly hooked. Henri was the skinniest but the tallest. Charles had a little more meat on him, with blue-green eyes that contrasted better with his olive skin than Henri's gray eyes did with him. While the clothes and watches they wore with casual indifference probably cost more than the typical Parisian's monthly salary, Clémence would probably not have guessed they were heirs to a multimillion dollar publishing empire had she seen them walking down the street.

Henri, she'd already met before her party, as he'd been dating Madeleine for some time, and Madeleine had told her plenty about him, since she was expecting an engagement ring any day now. Henri was a bit lazier than his alpha brothers, and he dragged his feet in terms of his career, so it wasn't a surprise that he'd take forever to propose, as well.

Charles, like Cesar, was a shameless flirt. He complimented Clémence as they drank and chatted, with such casual smoothness that she didn't feel awkward or put on the spot. He was simply appreciative of the feminine form, but with a twinkle in his eyes. He'd probably been flirting with Madeleine, too, and received humorous interference from Henri, which was what Clémence had witnessed from her birthday party.

Clémence heard from Celine that she and Charles had hit it off. The day after, they'd gone out for a drinks in the evening, where Charles commiserated to her about Cesar's death. It made sense that they would get along. Celine was boy crazy, and Charles seemed like a playboy. Both were flirts, and neither seemed to be looking for anything serious at the moment.

"I'm sorry about what happened to Cesar," Clémence said, taking a sip of her scotch.

"Well." Charles looked down at his glass. "Cesar made his decision. I'm disappointed in his actions, but what can you do? It was his choice."

Henri slowly shook his head. "I'm still having a hard time accepting it. Was it really a suicide? I looked up to Cesar." He looked to Charles. "We both did. He was always so full of life, so happy to be alive. He was the one who was always asking me to hang out and do fun things with me. Go on vacation at the last minute. Go to football games, clubs, skiing. He was up for anything."

Charles shrugged. "Maybe he had those moments. The truth is, he kept a good front. I wasn't going to get into this, but maybe this will help you understand, Henri." He took another sip of his drink before proceeding. "When Cesar was sixteen, he had a girlfriend. He was crazy in love with her and they went out for about eight months before she died in a freak car accident. You were probably too young to remember, since you were only ten, but did you notice anything off about Cesar at the time?"

"Well." Henri thought about it. "I did remember that Cesar was a bit gloomy sometimes. Now that you mention it, I did ask him once why he was so sad, and he told me he had a friend who died, but he didn't elaborate."

"Diane was her name," Charles said. "I was fourteen, and I'd met her a few times. She was nice.

She was from Guinea, and Cesar wasn't sure how our parents would have reacted if they had found out that he was dating a black girl. Not that they're racist." He shifted uncomfortably in his chair. "But they're...conservative." He took a sip of his drink. "It ate him up inside, Diane's death. He went to the funeral, but only I knew about it, and some of his friends from school."

"How exactly did Diane die?" Clémence asked.

"She was in the passenger seat of a car on the highway. A truck stopped short in front of them, and they crashed. Both of them died instantly."

"Wow. Cesar must've been upset. You think that caused his depression?"

"Sure," Charles said. "He changed after that. He partied harder and became more of a womanizer. I don't think he ever had a relationship that lasted more than three months again."

Madeleine put a hand over her heart. "I didn't know that about Cesar. That he was broken. Poor guy. At least now he's with Diane in heaven."

Nobody said anything for a moment. Clémence took a long sip of her scotch. The boys refilled their own drinks.

"So did Cesar see a psychiatrist about his depression?" Clémence asked.

"He must've, if he was taking antidepressants," Charles said.

"Did you know about the pills?"

"Yes. I caught him a few times taking them. When I asked him about it, he claimed they were vitamins, so I didn't think much of it. After all, Cesar was always going to the gym and was a bit of a health and fitness nut. When the police called us yesterday and told us that they found the pills in his bloodstream and that he'd overdosed from it, it made sense."

Henri stood up and walked over to the window. "Does it? He was having a great time at the party. The time of his life, in fact. He was dancing enough to rival that British guy, Ben. I mean, it doesn't make sense, at least to me. Cesar was the happiest guy I knew. Why would he suddenly decide to overdose on pills? He wasn't that drunk."

"I know you idolized him," Charles said. "We both did. But inside, there had always been this deep-rooted pain. Maybe the things he did, all the crazy stuff, all the fun he had, was all just been a distraction."

Henri shook his head. "It's a shame. And he was doing so well at his job. Profits were up seven percent so far this year in magazine sales, thanks to him."

"Yes. Papa was training him well. Now I'm going to have to take his place. I was so planning on going to law school and becoming a lawyer." Charles sighed.

"I see the car," Henri said, turning back to them. "My parents are here."

Chapter 9

*M*adame Laberg came out of the back seat of a black Mercedes. She was in her late fifties. Her shoulder-length brunette bob had bold white streaks. Dressed in a dark green Dior couture jacket and skirt, with beige heels and pearls around her neck, she wasn't unlike any other bourgeois housewife, but something about her was bold and direct. Her dark eyes were sharp, staring into Clémence's with an unnerving directness.

"Clémence Damour. You're just as pretty as your pictures." Madame Laberg broke out into a warm smile, which surprised Clémence. She greeted her with *bisous*. Then she kissed Madeleine. "And Maddie, as perfect as always. I apologize for being late. My husband was working late, as usual, at the company."

The man she was referring to was slowly getting out of the other side of the car, talking on the phone. He had a sturdy, bull-like build, like his two eldest sons, and he'd lost nearly all his hair.

Madame Laberg looked back at him and half-rolled her eyes. "My husband will probably be on the phone a while. Let's go to dinner, and he'll join us when he's free. Let's see what the chefs have cooked up tonight. I'm not even going to pretend I had a hand in this meal." She gave a little laugh.

The dining room had lots of high windows, allowing in plenty of light. In August, the sun set late in Paris, and the room was illuminated with the warm pink glow of the sunset. Madeleine sat beside Henri, while Clémence faced her. Charles sat beside Clémence. As the matriarch of the family, Madame Laberg sat at one end of the table, beside Clémence.

After making some small talk, Madame Laberg remarked to Clémence, "I hear you're dating someone."

Clémence turned to her in surprise. "Er, yes."

"That's too bad. You're precisely the kind of the girl Charles should be dating. He told me he was going out with a *hostess.*"

"Mother, please," Charles groaned.

Clémence smiled awkwardly. Madame Laberg was probably talking about Celine. Clémence didn't know what to say. Celine was one of her best friends.

"I'm just saying," Madame Laberg continued. "Those girls might be fun for the moment, but if you're looking for someone to stay with for life, especially at your age, you need to start looking for quality. Henri found someone. Look at Madeleine: beautiful, educated, with a career, and she's practically a fashion icon. So is Clémence. I heard about your kidnapping incident, dear. What a bother. You must've been traumatized."

"It's okay," Clémence said. "I've recovered."

"Clever girl, outsmarting your captors like that. You saved Madeleine's sister's life."

"It was luck." Clémence tried to brush it off.

"Modest too," Madame Laberg commented.

As a server poured wine for everybody, Monsieur Laberg finally arrived at the table and greeted everyone tersely. He sat down opposite Madame Laberg at the other end of the table.

"*Bonsoir*," Clémence said.

"This is Clémence Damour," Madame Laberg introduced. "I've invited her to dinner, *chéri*."

Monsieur Laberg's mind seemed to be a million miles away as he turned to Clémence, and seemed to be looking through her. "*Bonsoir*. Are you a friend of Charles's?"

"Yes," Clémence said, hesitantly, because he probably meant the question to ask whether she was Charles's new girlfriend.

"Clémence is great at solving mysteries," Madame Laberg said. "That's what Madeleine has been telling me. Clémence has been helping the Paris police with catching murderers."

"Really?" Charles looked at Clémence with interest.

"Perhaps she can help us," Madame Laberg said.

Monsieur Laberg's expression turned even more grave. "Why? As we discussed, the recent incident wasn't a murder."

"That's what you think," Madame Laberg said. "Our son did not kill himself. I strongly believe he was murdered. It's a mother's intuition."

Monsieur Laberg turned red, and he seemed to be holding back his anger in the presence of his guests.

"My condolences for your loss," Clémence said.

This was turning out to be an awkward dinner indeed. Luckily, two servers came in with their entrées.

"One of our chefs is from Thailand," Madame Laberg said. "So he experiments with Thai and French fusion."

"Oh." Clémence looked down at her small portion of pad Thai with peanuts sprinkled all over it. "This looks great, but I have a severe peanut allergy. I'm afraid I can't eat this. I'm sorry. I should've told you sooner."

"That's okay," Madame Laberg said. "Of course, we wouldn't want you to get sick. A peanut allergy—that's a bother. How serious is it?"

"In high doses, it can kill me," Clémence said. "But usually my throat clogs up a bit. This is why everything made at Damour is peanut free. My parents made sure of that growing up. Maybe it's one of the reasons Damour is so popular. There are a lot of people with peanut allergies."

"Maybe you can have a salad then?" Charles suggested, turning to the server. "Is that possible to get Clémence one of the chef's mango salads?"

"That sounds quite good," Clémence said.

"You have to try it. It's amazing."

"That was one of Cesar's favorites," Madame Laberg said sadly. "How could he have possibly...do that to himself? It's just not plausible."

"Accept it," Monsieur Laberg said. "Our son committed suicide. It's a fact. You found the suicide letter."

"But—"

"Just look at the facts. He was depressed. He was unhappy. He took the coward's way out." Monsieur Laberg shook his head. "I'm ashamed. I didn't raise him like that."

"You can't always look at the facts," Madame Laberg said. "Can you really think that your son, who has everything going for him, would just throw it all away? Is that really a fact to you?"

Her voice rose. She began to eat, chewing furiously. Clémence surmised that this had been an ongoing fight. The family seemed to be divided equally on this matter.

"It doesn't matter now," Monsieur Laberg said with control. "We all need to move on. Charles is going to be training to replace him. The company's going to be fine."

"It's not about work," Madame Laberg said with an exasperated sigh. "Not everything is *always* about work. Don't you care about your son?"

"I don't care to have this discussion in front of everyone." He stood up and threw his napkin down on his plate. "If you'll excuse me, I'm going to retire. I've lost my appetite."

Monsieur Laberg left as Clémence's salad arrived.

Chapter 10

*W*hile dinner had been delicious, Clémence could tell Monsieur Laberg wasn't the only one who'd lost his appetite. The rest of the meal was eaten in awkward silence and half-hearted attempts at conversation. After dinner, they had coffee back in the salon.

As the other three were busy arguing over the vinyls they wanted to play on the sound system, Madame Laberg sat next to Clémence on the couch. "I'm sorry for the evening, Clémence. I was trying not to lose my temper, but my eldest son is gone, and I'm going through a difficult time keeping things together."

She looked so sad and withdrawn that Clémence thought it would be appropriate to put an arm around her. "It's okay. It's normal to be mourning your son."

"It was embarrassing to fight with my husband in front of you and Madeleine. It's not dignified, and I apologize."

"It's really okay. Every family fights. How are the funeral arrangements going?"

"We're having problems with our priest. I insist that it's not a suicide, but he doesn't buy it, and he's not allowing the funeral to be held in the church that we go to."

"That's terrible."

"Yes, but what can we do?"

"Why do you think your son was murdered?" Clémence asked.

"A mother just knows. I guess it sounds pretty silly, huh?" She sighed. "Maybe I'm just delusional. Cesar was always a bright spot of sunshine in my life."

"Is it true that he was prescribed pills for depression?"

"Yes. Cesar had been seeing a psychiatrist, but only recently. About two months ago. He'd been overworked. Being the heir of *Editions Laberg*, primed by your successful, workaholic father since birth to take over the company, can have its toll on you. As far as I know, it wasn't serious. Sometimes, people need a bit of a boost—you know, to get them through the day? I personally take sleeping pills. He wasn't really depressed. It doesn't mean that he was suicidal."

Clémence nodded.

"And my husband—I'm sorry about his outburst earlier. He's just as upset."

"No need to apologize. It's not an easy time for either of you."

She stood up. "Come on. Why don't I give you a tour of the house?"

"I would love a tour."

They left Madeleine and the Laberg brothers on the couch, chatting over coffee. Madame Laberg showed her the backyard. As Clémence expected, there was the pool Berenice had described to her from the photo spread she saw in *Elle Decor*. The Mediterranean mosaic tiles, with the juxtaposition of futuristic white lounge chairs and plants cut in the shape of globes, gave the grand backyard an ethereal feel.

"We got a famed Spanish architect to redo the backyard," Madame Laberg said. "It's quite something, especially compared to the classical interior of the house."

"Which style do you prefer?" Clémence asked.

"Honestly, the outside, but my husband is traditional. He doesn't see the artistry as I do, but then again, he doesn't like to swim, either."

They went up the stairs, and she led Clémence into Cesar's room. It was more than just a bedroom. Double doors opened to a section that was more like an apartment. It was probably half the size of Clémence's parents' apartment. It contained a sizeable bathroom, a small salon that doubled as a library, and his bedroom.

"My husband wants to renovate this room right away." Madame Laberg shook her head. "Expand it into a guest room."

"He seems especially upset." Clémence examined the contents of Cesar's library, which doubled as his office. His work files were still on the table in ominous piles.

"Yes, I think he cares more—a lot more than he lets on," Madame Laberg said, looking sadly at Cesar's things. "That's always been his trouble. He doesn't know how to express any emotion except anger. Even that he tries to suppress. Personally, I think he feels guilty."

"How come?"

"He has always put a lot of pressure on his sons, particularly Cesar, because he was the oldest. And Cesar always complied. He was the top of his class, and he moved up the ranks of the company in a short amount of time. Cesar was working long hours, and he was good at it. But was he happy? He never had a say in his future, but he never complained about it. Cesar really wanted to please his father, but my husband is not the kind to dole out compliments easily. My husband works too much. Tonight, I had to go pick him up and drag him out of the office because you and Madeleine were over."

Clémence nodded. It was understandable that Monsieur Laberg would feel guilty if he felt that his actions had drove his son to suicide. He might have felt he'd pushed his son over the edge. But was Madame Laberg right? Had it been murder?

"Did Cesar have any enemies?"

"Enemies? Well that's something I've been wondering. Honestly, I'm sure there were many senior execs that were jealous and resentful that a young man would soon be their boss. It came with the territory. To think one of them would be responsible for his death..." She sat down, unable to bear the weight of her distress.

"So you really don't think Cesar could have taken his own life?" Clémence asked.

"Do you think I'm fooling myself?" she asked Clémence weakly. "Maybe I'm in denial, too. I just can't accept that my son would kill himself, like the way my husband can't believe that someone would kill him."

"Did you say you found Cesar's letter?"

"Yes. I was in his room, and I found it tucked under this pile of files." She pointed to the brown folders that were in a stack on the left of the table.

"I know the police have it now," Clémence said. "But do you happen to remember what it said?"

"I have a copy, as a matter of fact," Madame Laberg said.

"Oh, really?" Clémence tried to contain the excitement in her voice.

"Yes. It's in my study. My husband doesn't know I have it. I took a picture of it before the police came."

"Are you sure it was written by Cesar? Are you sure it was his handwriting?"

"Unfortunately, yes. The police informed us yesterday that the graphologist confirmed it. It was undoubtedly Cesar's writing, I'm sure of that. What I'm not sure of, however, is if it's a will, as the police seem to believe."

They walked to up the stairs to the third floor, where the entire floor belonged to the Monsieur and Madame Laberg. She opened one set of doors to her library. Three walls of the shelf were filled with books, and two of them were specially dedicated to books and magazines from *Editions Laberg*.

Madame Laberg looked through the bottom drawer of her desk in her study. "Here it is." She gave Clémence the printed photograph of the letter.

Clémence took it and read it silently to herself.

I leave my entire fortune, minus 10%, to be split equally among my father, mother, and brothers, Charles and Henri. The 10% goes to charity, for

Mothers Against Drunk Driving. My apartment in the 2nd arrondissement goes to Charles, and my Lamborghini goes to Henri.

Cesar dated and signed the bottom of the letter. It was the same night as the party.

"This is the suicide letter?" Clémence asked.

"That's what they're calling it. Don't you think it's just a will? Perhaps Cesar wrote it to be practical. He was the most practical of all my sons. Just because he was thoughtful enough to write a will, it doesn't mean that he meant to kill himself."

She could see Madame Laberg's point. The letter made no mention of hurting himself or why he would commit suicide.

Then again, why would Cesar write it and sign it on the night of the party? He might've been in a rush to get things taken care of. But the suicide would then be the clear-headed calculation of someone who'd planned out the evening.

Why would he kill himself? And why would he do it at the party, of all places? Was it really for attention? What point could he possibly have wanted to make by a public suicide? Something still didn't add up for Clémence.

Chapter 11

By the next afternoon, Clémence concluded that she agreed more with Monsieur Laberg and Charles than she did Madame Laberg and Henri. It seemed like the rational choice.

Cesar Laberg had lost a girlfriend at a very young age, and he'd been nursing a wound into his adult years. In fact, he pined for her so much that he had been relentless in pursuing Maya, who shared similar physical traits to his deceased ex. Cesar made up for it—or tried to distract himself, rather—with achievements, working hard in school and at his family's company. But the lingering sadness must've been dormant until recently, when he realized he was living an empty lifestyle, with no purpose and no love. From what she'd heard from the brothers, Cesar had been partying extra hard in the recent weeks up to his death.

Perhaps his lifestyle had been so empty and numbing that he'd felt that taking his life was the only logical thing to do. Since the love of his life had died, and he faced a lifetime of empty partying and a workaholic lifestyle, he was ready to end it. So he drew up a quick will and looked forward to a good night, where he would end up in a restroom from after overdosing from his antidepressants, pills that hadn't helped his depression as much as he probably would've liked. At least he got to spend the last moments of his life in good company.

Cased closed, right?

It had to be. Clémence didn't know what else she could do. It wasn't as if any of the employees from Laberg, the colleagues who were jealous of him, had been invited to the party. And the pills had been found in Cesar's jacket pocket.

Clémence just had to accept that it was suicide. Perhaps she'd just been used to the murders that'd taken place in Paris for the past few months—and solving them. She just had to accept that this instance wasn't a murder and to leave it alone.

She sipped her espresso in Damour's employee break room. She was the only one on break—not that she'd been working, really. She had been too busy mulling over the case to work properly in the kitchen, and she excused herself altogether after making a mediocre batch of mango macarons. Whenever she was in detective mode, she found it a challenge to get creative in the kitchen. She was a believer that your mood got transferred into whatever you were making, and her desserts could be sweeter if she baked on a day she was happy. She'd been in the break room since lunch, going over everything she knew about the case that she'd written down in her notebook.

Even with the new conclusion that she forced herself to accept, the case didn't feel quite closed. Was it because she, like Madame Laberg and Henri, just couldn't accept the fact that Cesar was dead?

Celine came in, dressed in her usual hostess uniform of black pants and a light lavender dress shirt.

"*Ça va*, Clémence? You're looking especially pensive today. Is everything okay?"

"No, it's fine. I'm just trying to digest how and why Cesar committed suicide."

"Oh. Right. So you confirmed it's not a murder?"

"Well, I don't know if 'confirmed' is the right word, since nobody can confirm anything. But the facts definitely point to suicide."

"That's a shame." Celine pulled up the chair beside her. "Charles must be going through hell right now. Didn't you say you were going to their house? Did you have dinner with them last night?"

"Yes." Clémence recalled how Madame Laberg had spoken about Celine. *Just a hostess.* Clémence wanted to change the subject.

"So how was it?" Celine asked. "Was their house as nice as Berenice kept going on about?"

"It was pretty cool, I mean, just as nice as the other mansions in Neuilly," Clémence said.

"How was Charles? Did he ask about me?"

"Oh, are you still going out with Charles?" Clémence asked.

She shrugged. "I have to say, I'm liking him a lot."

"But you always say that about every guy you go out with. You like them for a week, then you totally get over it as soon as you meet someone cuter."

"I know, but he's different. What's not to like? He's so smart, and he makes me feel, well, sexy and beautiful, you know? And he's sexy and beautiful, not to mention rich. I don't know what else I would want."

Clémence smiled politely. Charles hadn't mentioned Celine at all—but then again, he wouldn't, in the presence of his disapproving mother. "I didn't talk to Charles that much. My objective was to get more information on Cesar. If you had asked me, I would've grilled Charles about you."

"Oh, no!" Celine exclaimed in horror. "Don't do that. I want to play it cool. He hasn't called or texted recently, but I want to be patient and not mess this up. He's probably going through a lot right now, helping out with funeral arrangements, so it makes sense that he'd be too busy to do something again so soon."

"Yes, it's been messed up for the Labergs, and I think Charles is dropping out of law school so he could start working at *Editions Laberg* with his father."

"Right, and that's eating up his time."

Clémence wanted to warn Celine that Charles was a bit of a flirt, but she bit her tongue. What if he agreed with his mother that Celine was simply someone to fool around with, but not to be with long term? She didn't want to see her friend get hurt.

Clémence's cell phone rang. It was from an unknown number. She thought about not answering it. Not long ago, she'd been harassed by reporters grilling her about her kidnapping incident, so much that she almost changed her number, but they'd cooled off lately.

Her curiosity got the better of her, and she answered it. "*Allô?*"

"Clémence Damour?" A male voice, low and muffled came from the other line.

"*Oui.* Who is this?"

"I have information on Cesar Laberg's murder."

"What? Really, who is this?" Clémence demanded.

"Meet me at Chez Georgina in fifteen minutes, and I'll tell you everything."

Click.

Chapter 12

She hadn't recognized the voice at all. While it was distinctly male, she got the impression that it had been distorted to be indistinguishable.

Whoever it was claimed that Cesar was indeed murdered. Clémence couldn't pass up the opportunity to meet this person and find out what kind of info he had. How did he know she was looking?

At first she thought about calling the police, but she quickly reconsidered. She didn't have time for that, and it might even be a hindrance to have them there. It would be safe to go on her own, since Chez Georgina was a wine bar in the 6th arrondissement and there would be other patrons around.

After she retrieved her purse, she went and flagged down a taxi. She was dying of curiosity. Was it somebody from the party? One of Cesar's coworkers? And how did this person know she was investigating?

Since many Parisians were away on vacation during this month, the streets were calm, without any heavy traffic. The taxi was able to pull up to Chez Georgina in ten minutes. The place was on a small side street, near Jardin du Luxembourg. It was a place that could've been easily missed, given the inconspicuous nature of the signage, or lack thereof. It was a hidden gem for locals, however, given their quality wine selection and lack of tourists.

Clémence had been at Chez Georgina a few times before. The place could get especially rowdy on Friday and Saturday nights, where the bar would be crowded with red-faced Parisians and the tables were cramped with wine lovers who could barely hold conversations over the noise.

Clémence entered through the maroon door. A doughy, balding bartender in his sixties greeted her as he polished wineglasses with a towel. She smiled and looked around to see if she recognized anyone. A couple chatting at the bar was so enraptured in their own conversation that they didn't even notice when she stared at their profiles. There was a young man with glasses, a scholar or writer type, sitting at a small table by the window, scribbling away in his notebook. He didn't glance up at her either. There were quite a few other people there, too, eating a late lunch, and nobody seemed to pay her any mind.

Her man wasn't there yet, it seemed. Clémence was a few minutes early, after all. She sat down at the only free table in the corner in the back of the place and waited while keeping an eye on the door.

She was near the unisex toilet, and as she mulled over the menu, it was quite unpleasant to hear the toilet flush and the customers going in and out through the beads hanging over the wall opening that led to the restroom.

Another five minutes passed. The waiter came by and asked her what she wanted. He was tall and stiff, looking vaguely familiar, but it was probably because Clémence had been served by him before. Clémence was torn between two types of red wines.

"They're both excellent," the tall waiter said. "But if you want, I'll make the choice for you."

"Okay. That way it's your fault if I don't like it," Clémence joked.

He came back a minute later and put the wineglass on the table, telling her that he went with the glass of *Côtes-du-Rhône*. Clémence smiled up at him. Sometimes, the waiters in Paris could be friendly.

She took a sip and waited. The wine was a bit bitter for her taste, but she didn't want to hurt the waiter's feelings by sending it back. She checked her phone. There was a text message from Arthur saying he missed her, to which she texted back her own sweet nothings.

The front door opened, and Clémence looked up. It was a friend she recognized from university.

"Sylvie?" Clémence stood up.

The woman was a redhead–artificially so, as she'd always been. At the sound of her name, Sylvie jerked her head to Clémence. Surprise contorted her mouth into an O. "Clémence? Clémence Damour?"

Sylvie rushed over to Clémence to hug her. She was dressed head to toe in pink. Since they'd met in art school, Sylvie had never been shy to stand out from the crowd. Lime bangles clacked on her wrists, and silver eye shadow was blended up to her eyebrows. Her big plastic neon orange purse knocked Clémence's wineglass from her table as the girls pulled apart.

"*Oh là là!*" Sylvie exclaimed. "I'm so sorry!"

The wine had splashed all over the wooden table. Their waiter had been busy attending to someone else, but the bartender came over with a rag.

"It's okay," the bartender said. He put the rag over the table, letting the wine soak it up. "Let me get you a new glass."

"Really?" Clémence said. "*Merci beaucoup, Monsieur. C'est gentil.*" When he left, she turned back to Sylvie. "What are you doing here?"

"I work right around the corner, so I'm a regular here," Sylvie said. "What about you?"

"Oh, I'm waiting for someone. Wait—it wasn't you, was it?"

"What do you mean?" Sylvie asked.

"Did you call me asking me to meet you?"

"No. I haven't seen you for years, and I don't even think I have your number."

"Oh." Clémence looked around again. Her caller hadn't shown up.

"You mean you don't know who you're meeting?" Sylvie asked.

"No. It's a bit of a long story."

Before Clémence could elaborate, she felt her throat closing up. She coughed, putting both hands around her neck. It felt as if her throat was being sealed, and she couldn't do anything about it.

"Wa-ter," she gasped.

"Water," Sylvie repeated. She tried to hold Clémence steady. "She said she wants water! Somebody!"

But before she could drink anything, Clémence was falling to the ground and then she saw pitch black.

Chapter 13

She had a rancid taste in her mouth when she came to. Which was odd, because she'd dreamt of eating mango and raspberry macarons, the new recipes she'd been working on. But even in her dreams she couldn't taste them. They were simply devoid of taste when she bit into them.

When she woke up, she found herself staring at a peeling cream ceiling. Her stomach felt as if somebody had stabbed her with a rack and left it there. Her head hurt, and her tongue felt fuzzy with that horrid taste. Was there a trace of her own vomit?

"Where am I?" Clémence asked no one in particular. Why was her voice so groggy?

She craned her head up and saw Arthur jumping out of his chair. Next thing she knew, he was by her side.

"Clémence? Are you okay?"

Berenice and Sebastien were there, as well, concern written on their faces—and so was Sylvie, her friend from university. What was she doing here?

"I don't know," Clémence asked "What happened?"

"You're at the hospital," Berenice said.

"Oh my gosh, it was so scary," Sylvie exclaimed. "One minute we were chatting, and the next you were falling to the ground. I thought you were dead!"

"I don't know what happened," Clémence said wearily. "I just feel like hell. What did the doctor say?"

"I'll go get him now." Sebastien went out.

"They ran some tests," Arthur said, "when you were unconscious. He'll tell you soon."

"What were you doing today?" Berenice said. "Sylvie told us you were at Chez Georgina to meet someone? Who?"

Clémence closed her eyes. The events of the day came back to her slowly.

"It's the strangest thing," Clémence said. "Somebody called me on my cell earlier today. It was an unknown number. A man told me to meet him at the wine bar because he had information on Cesar's murder. Yes, he actually said murder. Naturally I was intrigued. His voice was distorted, and I didn't know who he was, but I couldn't turn down the opportunity to find out."

"Oh, Clémence," Arthur groaned. "You can't just go off meeting strangers without telling anybody."

"I'm sorry. I thought it would be safe since we were meeting in a public place. But I still don't know why I fainted like that. The guy never came, did he?" Clémence looked at Sylvie.

"I don't know which guy you mean," Sylvie said. "There was such a big commotion when you fell, and then the ambulance came, so I don't know if this guy showed up or not."

Someone knocked on the door, then proceeded to enter. Sebastien came back in, followed by the doctor, a tall man with salt-and-pepper hair dressed in a white cloak.

"Mademoiselle Damour, how are you doing?" the doctor asked.

"I'm pretty perplexed, Doctor," she said. "What happened to me?"

He looked at his clipboard. "It seems you had an allergic reaction. I saw on your file that you have a severe allergy to peanuts, and peanuts were found in your bloodstream."

Clémence hadn't had a reaction like this since she was a kid, when they first discovered her allergy. Her symptoms had felt familiar, the closing of the throat, the dizziness. But it had never been so bad that she had passed out. "How could that be? I don't eat peanuts."

"What did you eat today?"

"Let's see." Clémence thought. "For breakfast, I just had a couple of pieces of baguette with butter, then I went to work. I ate lunch at Damour, where everything is peanut-free. The chefs know I have an allergy. I had salmon with a side salad."

"And you consumed nothing after that?"

"No. Except, I went to a wine bar and ordered a glass of red. There shouldn't be any peanuts in there, right?"

"Not in wine, no."

"And I only took a sip. Then my friend Sylvie came in, we chatted for a few minutes, and I passed out."

Clémence's friends looked to each other. *It must've been the wine*, they were all probably thinking.

"Thanks, Doctor," Berenice said. "Can please you excuse us?"

"Sure," he said. "Clémence, you're fine to go. Stay extra careful with what you eat. Sometimes peanuts can be hidden in unlikely places."

"Thanks, Doctor. I'll be more careful next time."

When he left, Clémence exclaimed, "Did someone try to kill me?"

"Are you sure you didn't eat anything else?" Sebastien asked. "Absolutely sure?"

"No. Nothing."

Sylvie nodded. "I was there. She didn't have anything else on the table, and I knocked her glass over."

"I haven't been snacking lately," Clémence added. "I've been trying to eat healthy, so I try not to snack unless I have to. The wine was enough for me."

"You had the reaction immediately after drinking the wine, is that right?" Arthur asked.

"Yes," said Clémence. "And I would've had more of it, if Sylvie hadn't knocked over the glass. I guess you saved my life, Sylvie."

Sylvie shook her head. "Wow. So your wine was poisoned?"

"It would make sense, wouldn't it?" Clémence said. "Maybe whoever called me didn't want to give me information. They just wanted me dead."

"Who knows about your peanut allergy?" Sebastien asked.

"A lot of people," Clémence said. "My family. Friends—you guys know. The staff at Damour. I wonder if it was ever written about in the tabloids. I mean, some of those articles reveal a lot about me. Maybe anyone could find out about this if they did a little research."

"We are definitely hiring a bodyguard this time," Arthur said.

"Yesterday at dinner with the Labergs, I did tell them I had a peanut allergy, so the whole family knew, and their entire staff, as well."

"You think it was one of them?" Arthur asked.

"I don't know." Clémence shook her head. "Why would they? But who knows? I can't think straight right now."

After a moment of reflective silence, Berenice said. "So it was someone who knew you were investigating Cesar's death. It's strange, because this morning you said you were sure Cesar committed suicide. If this person didn't try to kill you, you would've left the case alone."

"I have to call the police to tell them about this," Clémence said. "Arthur, can you please pass me my purse?"

He handed over her brown Chloe purse. When she opened it to look for her smartphone, she pulled out a wrapper.

"What's this—" It was a chocolate bar wrapper, the kind Clémence could never eat because she knew there were traces of peanuts in it. "It's true. Somebody was trying to make it look like an accident. They planted this wrapper in my bag to make it seem like I'd consumed peanuts."

Clémence started dialing for Inspector Cyril St. Clair, then she realized something. "The same thing probably happened to Cesar. Somebody poisoned his dessert with the pills he was taking, so when they did the autopsy, they'd find the antidepressants he was taking and write it off as a suicide!"

Chapter 14

Clémence and Arthur rode in a taxi that was following Inspector Cyril St. Clair's car. They watched as Cyril sloppily parked stopped in front of Chez Georgina. The inspector's long spidery legs stepped out onto the street first, followed by the rest of his lanky body.

Clémence refused to ever be in the same car as the inspector except under the most dire circumstances. The man had a bad case of road rage that she wanted no part in. She felt sorry for the members of his team, who had to deal with his nasty behavior on a daily basis. Although recently he'd been treating her with a smidge more respect. His snide insults decreased every time she solved another murder case.

Arthur got out first and went around to Clémence's side to help her get out. She was feeling a lot better. She was lucky she'd only taken a sip of the wine. If a sip had been enough to send her to the hospital, there was no question what would've happened if the klutzy Sylvie hadn't shown up.

They followed the inspector and two members of his team into the cozy wine bar. The same bartender was tending the bar and looked surprised to see the grim-faced inspector.

Cyril introduced himself with his usual arrogance and spoke about the incident that had happened earlier. He demanded to see the waiter who'd served Clémence.

The bartender was glad to see that Clémence was all right.

She thanked him, then reiterated Cyril's question. "Where's the waiter who was working here?"

"He's not a regular employee of mine," the bartender said. "His name is Jean, but he was just helping out. I didn't know him before today."

"What do you mean? How could you not know who he is if he's working here?" the inspector said.

"My regular waiter Anton didn't show up for the lunch rush. I had to serve everyone and run around like a chicken with its head cut off. One of my customers noticed and asked why there was no one else working, and I told him my dilemma. I'd tried reaching Anton, but he was an hour late, and his phone was off. So this customer, who introduced himself as Jean, offered to help. He said he used to work at a wine bar just like mine in Lyon and knew a lot about wine and gastronomy so I told him he could serve—I would handle the cash and the end of the shift, and I'd paid him in cash. I was really grateful because he did his job with more efficiency than Anton."

"He's probably the one who poisoned my wine with ground peanuts," Clémence said.

The bartender's eyes widened at the accusation. "What?"

"Yes. I went to the hospital because I had a peanut allergy, and we think he was the person who wanted me dead."

"But why?"

"That's what we're trying to find out. We don't know who he is, either, but I bet he offered to work for you just for the opportunity to poison me. What other information do you have about him?"

"He gave me his phone number, in case I ever need his help in an emergency again," the bartender said. "I actually offered him a job, but he said he was already working at the moment, and I assumed he meant in another restaurant." He gave them the number from his contact book.

"Check this number out," Cyril said to one of his officers, who left the bar to work on it immediately.

"I doubt it's a real number," Arthur said.

"I agree," Clémence said. "He wouldn't be stupid enough to use a traceable number, at least."

"What did he look like?" Arthur asked her.

"Tall. I remember he loomed over me," Clémence said. "I hardly paid attention to him, although I looked up at him once. He was probably in his early thirties. His face was quite forgettable: dark hair, dark eyes, a hint of stubble, average features."

"Yes," the bartender agreed. "He had a very quiet demeanor. He had been drinking at the bar by himself, just observing, before he offered to work. I rarely paid any attention to him before he spoke up. He was the type to blend in with the walls."

"But there was something familiar about him," Clémence said. "I'd seen him before. But I can't seem to put my finger on it."

Arthur had already hired two bodyguards from a company that came recommended by his mother. They worked in rotating shifts throughout the day. The first bodyguard, Michel, was currently guarding outside their apartment door.

The presence of a bodyguard gave Arthur peace of mind when they were home. Clémence wasn't sure how she felt about it yet. Having a hulking man following her around to babysit her was going to be a nuisance, but what choice did she have, if she wanted to stay alive until she caught the guy who'd tried to kill her?

In the salon, Clémence wasn't in the mood to drink wine to unwind, as they often did at the end of the day. She stuck to tea, and Arthur drank a *café*. She'd had enough wine for the day.

"Where have I seen this waiter before?" Clémence closed her eyes. She'd been asking herself the same question all evening, to no avail. Miffy, her fluffy white dog, jumped up into her lap. Clémence stroked her back, still pondering.

Her cell phone rang. It was Inspector Cyril St. Clair.

"I tracked down the waiter, Anton, who missed his shift," he said. "Apparently, he was mugged and knocked unconscious in an alley. That's why he didn't show up for work for the lunch shift."

"I bet he was beat up by the same guy who was posing as my waiter," Clémence said.

"He's still out there," Cyril warned. He hung up before he really started sounding like he cared for her safety.

So this guy had it all planned out. He had chosen the place to meet Clémence, and he had gone out of his way to attack an innocent waiter of the place in order to step in his shoes.

Why was he so familiar to her? Had she met him somewhere before at a social event? At a party? Or perhaps he really was a waiter?

A waiter...

A possibility hit her. She retrieved her laptop from her room and popped in the DVD of the security footage from her birthday party that Ralph had given her.

"Arthur, come look at this." She played through the footage, fast-forwarding to the bits where the waiter came into view.

The cater waiter who served Cesar the crème brûlée was also lanky, with dark hair and a nondescript face. She couldn't see his face for the most part, but she kept watching the tapes carefully for a moment when she could. Then she got it: a split second when he glanced up at the chandelier, squinting.

"Is it him?" Arthur asked.

"Yes, it's him!" Clémence took a screenshot of his fuzzy black-and-white face. "That's how I recognized him. I don't know him at all, but he was one of the waiters hired for my party. He's our guy."

Chapter 15

Clémence had sent Cyril the freeze-frame of the cater waiter. Although the photo wasn't crystal clear, at least it gave a clear outline of his facial features, and they didn't have to rely on a police sketch. In the black-and-white footage, the waiter's cheekbones looked cavernous, giving him a sinister effect that she haven't noticed in real life. She had shuddered when the picture came out, blown up, from her printer.

And to think she had liked the waiter, too, and she even shared a laugh with him.

Her second bodyguard, Guy, accompanied her to work that morning. Guy and Michel had both followed her request to look less like bodyguards, so Guy was wearing a simple blue polo shirt and faded jeans. The shift was an easy one—all he had to do was sit in a corner of the Damour *salon de thé*, sipping *cafés*. Clémence still thought having a bodyguard during the day was silly, but she didn't argue with Arthur, who had to work and felt guilty for not being at her side to protect her during the day.

The first thing she did when she came in was see Carolyn, the manager, in her office.

"Clémence, *bonjour*." Carolyn greeted her with *bisous*. "Are you okay? I heard you had an allergic reaction yesterday."

Clémence had asked her coworkers not to make a big deal of her incident. "I'm fine. I wanted to ask you, did you get the invoice from the catering company hired to work at my birthday party? Did you already pay them?"

"As a matter of fact, I did get it, and I was going to mail out the check later today."

"Thanks, Carolyn. Actually, I want to deliver the check in person. I want to speak to the boss."

"Sure." Carolyn looked into her "outgoing" tray on her desk and took out an envelope. "Here's the check."

"Who's the owner, again?" Clémence asked. "I met her at the party. Was it Pierrette something?"

"Pierrette Manteau."

"Right. Thanks. I'm off."

The catering company was in the 14th arrondissement, and they typically catered French cuisine for special events. Clémence had only hired them for the waitstaff, since her chefs and bakers at Damour had already provided the food.

She got off the Métro at Denfert-Rochereau with her bodyguard, Guy. They walked past the wraparound lineup for the Paris Catacombs, which she had visited when she was a teenager for a date with her first boyfriend. She hadn't found it as fascinating as her boyfriend had, however. The dead skulls lining the walls of the underground tunnels killed any romance that had been on her mind that day. She hadn't returned since.

Arthur had expressed interest in going, because he'd lived in Paris all of his life and he'd never been, but they never had the chance to because the line was usually an hour long. Perhaps they'd go in the off season, like in the late fall or winter.

As she followed the address of the catering company on the map on her smartphone, she and Guy found themselves in a secluded alley. She had to admit, good thing she had a bodyguard to accompany her to such places.

When she reached the right number, there was only an inconspicuous sign above a red door to advertise the place. All the windows were tinted. There was no sign of life anywhere. It was one of those sketchy kinds of alley where homeless men relieved their bladders.

She rang the doorbell. After about a minute, Pierrette Manteau answered. Pierrette had been present alongside her team at Clémence's birthday party. She was a woman in her early sixties with long white hair tied up into a bun, and she wore bifocals that magnified her eyes, making her appear loopy and eccentric.

"*Bonjour?*" Pierrette greeted her with a confused smile. Her orange-red lipstick was crackling over her dry lips.

"Madame Manteau, do you remember me? It's Clémence Damour. Your team worked at my birthday party last Saturday?"

"Oh, Clémence, of course! I'm sorry. Sometimes I'm so bad with names and faces."

Clémence chuckled. "It's fine. But a bit of a problem if you're bad with names *and* faces."

"I'll say. It seems to get worse with old age, too."

"This is Guy," Clémence said.

The bodyguard nodded and smiled at Pierrette.

"*Bonjour,*" Pierrette said.

"I was wondering if I could talk to you for a minute," Clémence said.

"Of course. Come on in."

They passed an industrial kitchen where three cooks were working. Clémence followed Pierrette into her office at the back. Guy stayed just outside the door.

It looked as if a yard sale had exploded in there. Useless knickknacks and souvenirs from various vacations were everywhere. They cluttered her desk, along with pictures of her family members and mountains of paperwork. The office was the size of a closet, and Clémence felt a bit claustrophobic.

"First of all, here's the check." Clémence pulled out the envelope and gave it to her.

"Thanks, dear. Again, I'm so sorry that a guest passed away that night. But it happens, I suppose."

"It's very unfortunate. Thank you, and tell your staff I appreciated their professionalism."

"It's no problem. In my thirty plus years in the industry, I have to say, this is not the first time I have witnessed a death on the job. Seven years ago, the CEO of a large oil company simply clutched his heart when he was in the middle of eating a piece of filet mignon and fell headfirst onto his plate. Heart attack. I'll never forget it."

"That's terrible."

"Anyway, enough of this awful talk. Was there anything else I could do for you, dear?"

"Well, there is one thing. You see, I was wondering if I can talk to one of your employees that worked that night. I have some questions to ask him."

"Who?"

"I don't know his name. But he's tall. He looks to be in his early thirties. Dark hair. Thin face. Here." Clémence pulled out the surveillance picture of the man.

"David? Oh. Actually he's a new hire. He had a lot of experience, and he did a great job that night. However, I've been calling him for other jobs, and his phone has been out of service. I even tried emailing, but the emails kept bouncing back. It's a bit strange."

"Strange indeed," Clémence muttered. "Do you have any other information on him? How did you hire him?"

"He called out of the blue, asking if there were any openings. As a matter of fact, there were, and I asked him to email me a CV. He insisted on delivering the CV himself, so I figured, why not check him out and interview him? He came and sat where you sat. He seemed very knowledgeable about food and wine. He even offered to work for free as a trial basis for our next job, which was your birthday party. David seemed like a very eager go-getter, and I couldn't refuse. Plus, we were short staffed anyway, since many of my waiters are on vacation. I told David that if he did a good job, I would give him the full wage, and I did."

"Do you still have his CV?" Clémence asked.

"Yes, it's here somewhere."

Clémence looked on as Pierrette searched her files. Somehow Pierrette was able to retrieve the CV in no time, which surprised Clémence. There must've been an order to the chaos, Clémence figured, otherwise, Pierrette wouldn't have been able to keep a reputable company running as smoothly as she did for so many years.

She handed the CV to Clémence.

David Hortense. His experience working for Parisian restaurants was a mile long. There was a picture of him. A clear headshot, where he was looking sternly into the camera. In France, it was legal to put a picture on a CV, unlike in the States, where Clémence had been surprised to learn from her American friends that it wasn't allowed.

Now that she had a clear color photo of him, she knew without a shadow of a doubt that he had been the one who had served her the wine, and thus he had been responsible for poisoning her.

"What else do you know about him?" Clémence asked.

"Is he in trouble?" Pierrette frowned.

"Well, we have reason to believe David Hortense is trouble. That is, if David is his real name, which I seriously doubt. He is the police's top suspect for the murder of Cesar Laberg."

"Murder? I thought Cesar committed suicide. I read that in the paper this morning."

"We have reason to believe that David was behind the death and tried to frame it as a suicide. I'm telling you because if you hear from David, please call me right away. I very much doubt he'll be in touch again, but just in case he does, be on guard."

"This is frightening. A murderer among my staff? I mean, I hardly knew him, but I just can't imagine!"

"It happens. Some people in this world are cunning and psychotic. We don't know what he wanted with Cesar, but we have to find out. Please think if you know anything else about him."

"Well," Pierrette said slowly. "I only saw him twice. The first time for the interview, and the second time for your birthday party. He brought his work clothes. Everybody had to wear white dress shirts and black pants. Usually it's something I can provide our servers, or reimburse them for their purchase, but he insisted he had his own, so he showed up already dressed. Our conversations for the rest of the evening were work related. He was polite to the staff, and took to the tasks quickly. I mean, it's not the most difficult job. Serve food and make the guests feel taken care of. I don't recall having a personal conversation with him at all. I figured I'd get the chance to find out more about him as we continued to work together."

"I see. Perhaps I can get the contacts of your other staff members? Maybe they have information on David."

"Sure. I can do that. I doubt that they'll have more to say, considering David seemed to be all business and I hardly saw him interacting with the other workers, even when they took breaks, but you can certainly try."

"Thank you, Pierrette."

Clémence took a picture of the CV, then a close-up of David's photo, and sent it to Inspector Cyril St. Clair.

Chapter 16

When Clémence returned to the Damour kitchen, she rewarded herself with a treat. She must've been more stressed than she would admit to herself, because she grabbed a fresh pistachio éclair, still warm from one of the cooling trays, and ate it in two bites. The murderer was still out there. She hoped Cyril and his team would find this guy soon, but she wasn't exactly optimistic. She imagined herself shadowed by a bodyguard for the foreseeable future.

"Hey, Clémence," Sebastien said. "Did you find out anything new?"

"Sort of," she said. "This picture." She showed Sebastien the CV. "Do you remember this guy at all?"

Sebastien examined the photo. "Hmm. He does look familiar. But I have to admit, I wasn't really paying attention to the waitstaff that night."

"It's creepy. He's in the background, yet he has eyes and ears everywhere. A chaotic party is the perfect place to slip something in someone's food or drink to kill them. Who is this guy? I rewatched the surveillance footage again. He spoke to Cesar. What was he saying to him?"

"Was he talking to anyone else at the party?"

"No. Not from what I could tell from re-watching the surveillance footage anyway. It would make sense that this guy would go out of his way to charm Cesar. Maybe he was talking up the crème brûlée. I just hope the police will figure something out."

"Yes," Sebastien agreed, but he sounded doubtful, as well. The police didn't have the best reputation. Crimes in the city often went unpunished. Pickpockets were all over the place, and so were robbers and thieves. Clémence couldn't rely on the police to solve this murder.

Celine came in. "Hey. It was super busy up front, Clémence, so I couldn't talk to you, but I'm on a break. Did you go somewhere? Your bodyguard is super hot, by the way. Is he single?"

"Oh, Celine. I thought you were stuck on Charles?"

"He never got back to me," Celine said. "Too bad, because I was willing to be a shoulder for him to cry on. I texted him last night, and the night before. Even if he's grieving, he'd at least text me back. I thought he liked me, but I guess I was wrong. I sure can pick them, right?"

Clémence recalled what Madame Laberg had said about Charles dating a hostess. For a guy who still lived at home and obeyed his parents when it came to his career, it wasn't a surprise that Charles would obey his mother in terms of his love life too. "You're too good for Charles."

"Yeah. And the easiest way to get over one guy is to get on top of someone else."

"Sure, I can ask Guy whether he's single." Clémence smiled at her wryly. "Hey, do you recognize this guy?"

Clémence showed her David Hortense's photograph on the CV.

Celine examined it. She frowned. "This guy does look familiar."

"He was a cater waiter at my party," Clémence said. "Nobody seems to know his real identity. Do you remember him at all from the party?"

"I don't think the party's where I recognized him. I've seen him somewhere else. I just don't remember where at the moment."

"I believe he's responsible for Cesar's death."

"And he tried to kill you?"

Clémence nodded.

Celine closed her eyes to think. "I know I've seen that face before," she muttered.

Sebastien and Clémence stared at Celine as she tried to think.

"Anything?" Sebastien asked after a long minute had passed.

Celine still didn't answer. She closed her eyes to rack her brain. After another minute, her eyes sprang open. "I got it! Okay. You know how I went out for drinks with Cesar at the Buddha Bar?"

"*Oui*," Clémence said.

"Well, at the end of the evening, he paid for the bill. Charles said he'd take me home, and we were about to leave when he got a call, and he excused himself to take it outside. At first I waited at the table, but I figured since we were ready to go, I'd go outside and have a cigarette. He was outside. His car had pulled up—I knew it was his car because he'd picked me up. A man got out of the car. I remember thinking that he was kind of cute, too, if a little tall. He was dressed well and had a tough look to him. Charles was talking to him, I presumed about business. I'd finished my cigarette when the car drove off. I didn't want Charles to think I was spying on him, so I went back in and sat back at the table. He said that he had to get me a cab instead because he had some last-minute work to attend to. I was disappointed, but Charles was pretty gracious about it and paid for the cab in advance."

"Are you sure this was the same guy that was talking to Charles?"

"I think it is. I mean, maybe I didn't notice him when he was working at the party, but dressed in the suit, he was more striking, and I had a good look at him. I've always liked tall, lanky guys."

"What kind of guys don't you like?" Sebastien joked.

Celine playfully punched him on the arm. "I'm pretty sure it was the same guy, Clémence."

"So. This guy is connected to Charles. He came out of Charles's car?"

"I think so. Charles has a driver, so this guy came out the back seat. He and Charles had an intense chat."

Clémence jumped off her stool and paced as she thought about it. "I think he's working for Charles. Charles hired him to kill his own brother."

Sebastien and Celine looked at her and then at each other.

"So Charles was the one who wanted me dead," Clémence said. "It all makes sense."

Chapter 17

*I*nspector Cyril St. Clair was looking more dapper than usual. In a dark suit with a pale blue silk pocket square, he looked as if he was going to a wedding. He was dressed for victory. Clémence and Arthur followed him and a few members of his team into the *Editions Laberg* building in the 6th arrondissement.

"Can I help you?" the receptionist asked when they entered.

"We're here to see Charles Laberg," Cyril commanded. "*Now.*"

The woman narrowed his eyes at him, but not one to argue with the police, she said coldly, "Second floor, third door on your left."

Cyril didn't thank her and simply led the way upstairs.

Charles's office door was already open, and he was talking on the phone when they entered. Clémence thought she saw his eyes widen in fear at the sight of them, but he simply held a finger up, signifying that he would be free in a minute.

When he hung up, he smiled at the inspector. "Gentlemen. Is there a problem?"

"Charles Laberg," Cyril started. "You're under arrest for the murder of Cesar Laberg."

Two police officers handled the job of handcuffing him.

"Get my father," Charles said coolly to the employees who had begun to gather outside the office to see what was going on. "I'm innocent. This is ridiculous. What is this farce?"

"You killed your brother and you tried to kill me," Clémence said, stepping forward. "Your so-called employee, Guillaume Roussy, confessed to everything."

"What?" There was a flash of fear in Charles's eyes again—Clémence was sure of that now—as her eyes locked into his.

"What's going on here?" Monsieur Laberg stormed in.

"Charles is being arrested for the murder of your late son," Cyril said.

Monsieur Laberg looked to Charles, who was vehemently shaking his head. "I did not kill my brother."

"That why did you employ Guillaume Roussy?" Clémence asked.

"Who is this Guillaume Roussy?" Charles said. "I don't know who you're talking about."

"Maybe you know him by one of his many aliases," Clémence said. "Jean? David Hortense? You hired him to do your dirty work, didn't you? After all, he's been living off the grid. When we identified Guillaume's real identity, the police confirmed my suspicions and traced him to you. He's on your payroll. What other jobs could possibly be worth a six-figure transaction other than murder? Guillaume has already been arrested, and he confessed."

"He's lying!" Charles's face was stony, but a vein began to pulse at one temple.

"Why would he? Why else would he be on your payroll?"

"Son?" Monsieur Laberg looked at Charles with a mixture of confusion and horror.

"She's lying," Charles said to him. "This girl is nothing but a pathetic amateur detective."

"You tried to kill me," Clémence said. "Your father was at the dinner. He'd remember. Monsieur Laberg, remember when I said I was allergic to peanuts? Your son hired someone to poison my wine at a wine bar with ground peanuts. Charles feared I was getting to close to his cover-up. That was your mistake, Charles. I wouldn't have suspected you if you hadn't blatantly tried to kill me. You almost succeeded too, if there hadn't been an accident with the wineglass."

"Really," Charles persisted, even though his face was flushed red. "I have no idea what you're talking about."

"You wanted your brother dead. He was the heir to *Editions Laberg*, and you couldn't stand it. You enrolled yourself in law school in an attempt at a respectable career, but you hated it, and your marks were average at best. Your other choice was to work at your father's company and work your way from the bottom up, which you didn't want to do. Your brother, on the other hand, had been primed from birth to take over the company." Clémence walked closer to Charles. "You hated him for that. He was superior to you in every way. More handsome. More confident. Always got your parents' attention. Always got the girl. And you got the short end of the stick every time."

"Father didn't even give me a chance at the company," Charles spat out. "It was always Cesar who got everything. And Cesar was pathetic. He was always going on about his lost love. It got so boring. I figured I was doing him a favor by killing him."

"So you planted a rough draft of his will in a conspicuous place to make his death look like a suicide."

"Bravo." Charles sneered.

"You got what you wanted for a while," Clémence said. "You got his office, his position. But it's all over now. You're going to rot in jail for the rest of your life."

The police took Charles out. Monsieur Laberg sat down at the desk, the look of utter shock still on his face. He buried his face in his hands. One son was dead, and the other one would be in jail. He might have built an empire, but he'd lost two sons in one fell swoop.

Chapter 18

"Poor Celine," Clémence said. "She still can't seem to get over the fact that she fell for a murderer."

"She has pretty bad taste in men in general," Sebastien stated bluntly.

Clémence tried not to laugh, as Celine'd had a huge crush on Sebastien only months ago.

"At least they only had an innocent drink date and not a full-blown relationship," Clémence added.

Clémence, Arthur, Sebastien, and Maya were on their first double date at La Coquette, a chic restaurant close to Damour.

"I'm just glad the whole thing's over," Maya said, digging into her escargot with a special fork. "And it's now obvious that I had nothing to do with Cesar's death."

"I'd still date you if you were a murderer," Sebastien joked.

"You wouldn't." Maya playfully ribbed him with her elbow.

"But I think I know why Cesar used to be so taken with you," Clémence said. "When he was sixteen, he had a girlfriend who died in a car crash. He'd been pining for her since. When I was over at the Laberg house, I snooped around his house a bit and a found a little photograph of her in his desk."

"Did she really look like me?" Maya asked.

"Well, she had the same mocha skin, freckles over her nose, and similar corkscrew hair," Clémence said. "Your features are a bit different, and I wouldn't say you were twins or anything."

"Oh good. It would be weird to be someone's doppelgänger."

Arthur hadn't been speaking because he'd been busy with his eggplant appetizer with sesame sauce and cheese. "Have you tried this? It's really the best."

He cut Clémence a piece, and she chewed. "It's got this great smoky texture."

"Definitely original. The chef changes the menu practically every week." La Coquette was a Michelin-starred restaurant.

"Any vacation plans?" Clémence asked the other couple.

"I have to visit my family in Marseille," Maya said. "But Sebastien and I are probably going to spend a few days in Saint Tropez. What about you guys?"

"First we're going to Normandy," said Arthur. "Our family has a little house there."

"Little?" Clémence arched an eyebrow.

"It's modest compared to the houses around it. Anyway, we'll probably spend about a week there, before we get bored. Then we'll go to Amsterdam for a week."

"Amsterdam?" Sebastien gave Clémence a wry look. "What trouble are you going to get up to there?"

"No trouble," Clémence said. "Just innocent fun. No drugs, no prostitutes. Only bike riding and looking at windmills."

Arthur laughed. "Since the Netherlands is so small, we're going to check out a lot of cities around the country."

"Sounds great," Maya said. "Be sure to check out Utrecht. It's so charming, and it's got a great church."

"It's on our list," Clémence. "And fingers crossed that no murders will follow us there."

"Who knows," Sebastien said. "Maybe the Dutch police can use your help over there."

Clémence laughed. "I hope not. I mean, I really, really hope not. Summer's not going to last for long. It's already the second week of August! I want to enjoy it for once, and not have to chase after murderers and almost get killed in the process. I'm glad that bodyguards aren't necessary anymore."

"Well, I'm actually doubling as Clémence's bodyguard these days," Arthur said. "There's a gym at my work, so I've been getting ripped for the position."

He flexed his bicep, and Clémence groaned, smacking his arm down. "Oh, spare us."

Two waiters came by with their entrées.

"There are no peanuts in these meals, right?" Clémence asked them for the second time, just to make sure.

"None whatsoever," the waiter insisted.

"Thanks."

Arthur squeezed her hand. Clémence knew she was being paranoid, but they understood. She suddenly felt a surge of happiness being with people she loved and enjoying their company. She had been so close to death, after all. But it was time to let any remnants of fear go, to fully enjoy the present.

"Come on," Clémence said. "Let's dig in."

Recipes

Recipe #1

Classic Crème Brûlée

Crème brûlée is a classic French dessert of a custard topped with caramelized sugar. It's easier to make than you think. You will need a mini blowtorch to caramelize the sugar. If you don't have a mini blowtorch, I find that the crème brûlée also tastes delicious even without the crust.

Makes 4.

Ingredients:
- 1 3/4 cups heavy cream
- 1 tsp pure vanilla extract
- 4 large egg yolks
- 1/4 cup + 3 tsp granulated sugar
- Pinch of salt

Adjust rack to center and preheat oven to 300°F. Bring a teakettle of water to boil. In a baking dish, put in 4 ramekins (5 or 6 oz., about 3 inches in diameter and 1.74 inches deep). The baking dish should be as deep as the ramekins.

Pour cream into a small saucepan. Bring the cream to a simmer over medium heat, then remove the pan from the heat. Cover and let it sit for about 10 minutes.

In a mixing bowl, combine 1/4 cup sugar, egg yolks, and salt by lightly whisking them together. Set aside.

Use a candy thermometer to check the temperature of the cream. Make sure it's no higher than 165°F. If it is, let it cool to 165°F before the next step.

Lightly whisk 1/2 cup of the cream into the yolk mixture. Stir for about 30 seconds, to temper the yolks. Then gently whisk in the remaining cream, stirring for about 15 minutes. Do this lightly to make sure the mixture is not frothy. Stir in vanilla.

Place a fine sieve over a heatproof bowl. Pour the mixture through the sieve to strain out any solids.

Divide the mixture evenly among the 4 ramekins in the baking pan. There will be a bit over an inch of custard in each ramekin, and it shouldn't come all the way to the rim.

Put the baking pan in the center of the oven. Put a piece of aluminum foil over the pan. Bake custards until center is slightly jiggly, like Jell-O, which can take from 40 to 55 minutes. Test it by reaching into the oven with tongs and shaking one of the ramekins gently. If it responds with a wavelike motion instead of a jiggle, it's not done yet. After 5 more minutes, check again. They should not be brown.

Be careful when removing the baking pan from the oven. Take the ramekins out of the water safely using a slotted spatula or tongs wrapped with rubber bands (if they don't have rubber handles). Transfer the ramekins onto a rack.

Let the ramekins cool at room temperature for 30 minutes, then transfer (uncovered) to the refrigerator to cool completely. Once they are refrigerator-cold, wrap each ramekin with plastic wrap.

Refrigerate at least 2 hours or up to 3 days before caramelizing. After you take the ramekins from the fridge, set them on a work surface. Sprinkle 1/2 to 1 tsp of sugar over each one. The more sugar you add, the thicker the crust will be. You may need to tilt and tap the ramekin to even out the sugar layer. Wipe any sugar off the rim.

For best results, use a mini blowtorch. Hold the torch flame 2 to 3 inches away from the top and slowly glide it back and forth over the surface until the sugar melts. It should turn a deep golden brown. Allow sugar to cool and harden for a few minutes. Serve it immediately, before the sugar softens and gets sticky.

The great thing about this is that you can make the custard in advance, and later get it ready for serving by making the crust.

Recipe #2

Orange Crème Brûlée

A simple adaptation to the original Classic Crème Brûlée recipe. After the cream comes to a simmer, remove from heat and add the ingredients below:

- 1 tbsp Grand Marnier or triple sec
- 2 tsp finely grated orange zest
- only 1/2 tsp vanilla extract (omit 1 tsp vanilla from original recipe)

Cover and let sit for 10 minutes.

Recipe #3

Café au Lait Crème Brûlée

Omit vanilla extract from the Classic Crème Brûlée recipe.

After cream comes to a simmer, remove from heat and whisk in 1.5 teaspoons of instant espresso powder, until dissolved. Cover and let sit for 10 minutes.

Recipe #4

Ginger Crème Brûlée

Omit the vanilla extract from the Classic Crème Brûlée recipe. Instead, add 1/2 tablespoon of firmly packed finely grated fresh ginger to the cold cream before bringing it to a simmer.

Recipe #5

Earl Grey Tea Crème Brûlée

Omit the vanilla extract from the Classic Crème Brûlée recipe. After the cream comes to a simmer, remove from heat and immediately add 5 Earl Grey tea bags. Prod bags with a spoon to submerge them. Cover and let sit for 10 minutes.

Recipe #6

Lemon Crème Brûlée

Omit the vanilla extract from the Classic Crème Brûlée recipe. Pour 1 tablespoon of fresh lemon zest into the cream before bringing it to a simmer. Remove from heat. Cover and let sit for 10 minutes.

Recipe # 7

Lavender Classic Crème Brûlée

The perfume of the lavender with a hint of vanilla gives this dessert the feel of Provence. Make sure to only buy lavender suitable for culinary use.

Adapt the crème brûlée recipe by adding 1 tablespoon of dried culinary lavender to the cream before bringing it to a simmer. Remove it from the heat. Allow to cool for 45 minutes. Pour the lavender-infused cream through a fine-mesh sieve into a clean bowl and set aside.

About the Author

Harper Lin lives in Kingston, Ontario with her husband, daughter, and Pomeranian puppy. The Patisserie Mysteries draws from Harper's own experiences of living in Paris in her twenties. When she's not reading or writing mysteries, she enjoys hiking, yoga, and spending time with her family. She is currently working on more cozy mysteries.

www.HarperLin.com

32464812R00088

Printed in Great Britain
by Amazon